Advance Pr...

"... a delightfully action-pac[k]
With smooth writing, good c...
any video game, 'Fyrelocke'...
grade on up ...
—Mallory Forbes (Mallory Heart Reviews)

"Fyrelocke is a very fast paced novel. [...] I finished this book in a single afternoon. I enjoyed it immensely. [...] I would recommend Fyrelocke to anyone who enjoys easy to read but very hard to put down books."
—Alex McGilvery (www.celticfrogreviews.com)

"Oh me...oh my...such a fun and adventurous book this was! [...] I can only hope that there will be a Book Two soon...really soon!"
—Patty Magyar (Books, Thoughts and a Few Adventures...)

"... a simply charming and captivating book where anything goes and the characters are goofy enough to make you grin!"
—Dianne Bylo (tometender.blogspot.com)

"... fast paced from the very beginning, it is filled with twists and turns you just don't see coming ..."
—Shelly Hammond (GoodReads.com reviewer)

"Oh the fun. [...] Mayhem and magic are always a fun combination for great escapism and R. Christopher Kobb brings it."
—Michelle Auricht (www.novelsontherun.blogspot.com)

"Very well written, superb imagery, and a story that keeps you guessing till the end ..."
—Ramona Alba (headouttheoven.blogspot.com)

At the center of the cave was a small pool of water, clear and perfectly still. A constant drip echoed rhythmically, unseen in the stillness. In the middle was the source of the curious purple glow. Jack waded to it and spotted a rock, slightly smaller than a baseball—the source of the unnatural glow that filled the cavern. The driving, pulling sensation was stronger now, unrelenting.

He stooped to pick up the stone. His eyes grew wide as he brought it level with his nose. It began pulsing, a bright purple light. No sooner had he stood fully than a strange sensation thundered through him. His legs turned to jelly. His mind reeled.

Everything went black.

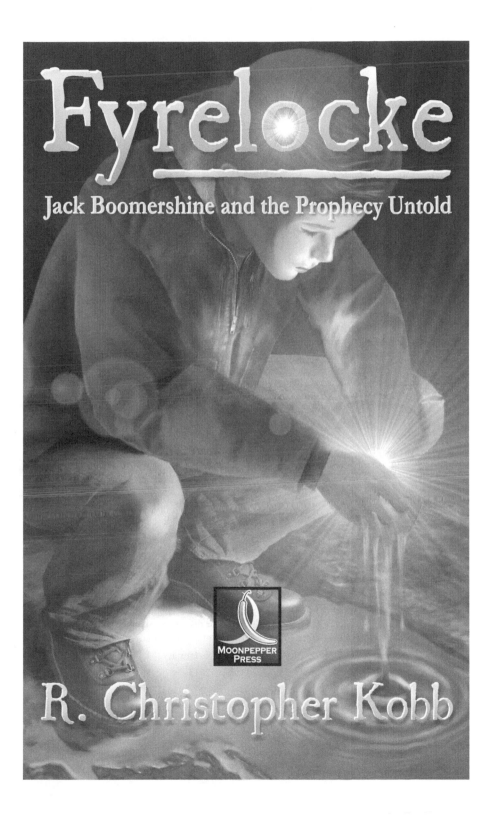

Fyrelocke

Jack Boomershine and the Prophecy Untold

MOONPEPPER
PRESS

R. Christopher Kobb

ISBN: 0989207201
ISBN-13: 978-0989207201

www.rckobb.com

Published by Moonpepper Press, 143 South Randall Road #19, Batavia, IL 60510, U.S.A. For sales and press inquiries call 888. 457. 7435.

Publisher's Cataloging-in-Publication data
Kobb, R. Christopher.
Fyrelocke : Jack Boomershine and the prophecy untold / R. Christopher Kobb.
p. cm.
ISBN 978-0-9892072-0-1
Series : Fyrestones
Summary : When a twelve-year-old inventor discovers a magic stone, he finds himself caught in the middle of an evil scheme.
[1. Magic --Fiction. 2. Inventors --Fiction. 3. Fantasy.] I. Series. II. Title.
PZ7.K78785 Fy 2013
[Fic] --dc23   2013936577

1 2 3 4 5 6 7 8 9

First Edition

DEDICATION

—

To all those who see the beauty
beneath, those who still believe in
magic, and those who can squint
and spot what the world lacks. To
dreamers everywhere.

Chapter One
The Bumbling Bus

J ack Boomershine sat at the back of the Flipper P. Bumbling school bus as it slogged to a field trip in the Cliffs of Brighton. He should have been trying to figure out how his jetpack had shot him into a tree on Argot's Hill the night before. Instead, he risked confiscation of his cell phone by openly staring in dumb confusion at it.

The cell phone had nothing to do with the jetpack, of course. That was the problem. Strapping a rocket to your back and shooting yourself through the air is a surprisingly tricky business—unless surviving is not a priority. The twelve-year-old inventor had survived the night before, but barely. Instead of using the bus ride to conduct post-crash analysis as he had planned, he puzzled at the strange text message that had suddenly appeared on his phone. For the fourth time, he read the message from *Anon1007*. Between the jostling of the bus and trying not to get caught with his phone out, he could not be certain he had read it correctly.

```
In the cave with your friends, as the
words "spiny and stubby" are spoken, you
must turn left.
```

A pothole jarred the bus. Tree-shaped bruises across Jack's ribcage screamed at him, and the windows shuddered in their frames. The two girls in the seat ahead squealed in harmony, but the noise nicely covered the phone's little ping, registering a second anonymous message.

```
Do not follow them. Turn left. Follow the
pull.
```

Jack did not understand this message any more than the first. *Follow the pull?* It had to be his best friend, Chase Lucre, playing tricks. Who else would text something like that? Chase had gone on this same trip with his own class two days before.

Jack pushed "Send" on his response, not a particularly nice one, but it promptly came back undeliverable.

He was impressed. Chase did not know computers very well. Jack was the inventor, the one who knew how to program and even hack them on occasion. He had no idea Chase knew you could send an untraceable message, let alone how. Maybe his friend was finally embracing the new millennium—and with a practical joke, maybe Jack's darker tendencies were starting to rub off on Chase.

Chapter Two

A Crystal in a Cave

⎯

The squealing girls got off the bus ahead of Jack and fell in with the throng of students milling about the front entrance to the caves. Thick October clouds roiled in the sky, and Jack's face tingled from the mist. He would have no chance for a second go at his jetpack tonight, even if he did figure out what had gone wrong.

He stepped from the bus directly into a puddle of mud. Mrs. Icky-Butt—Mrs. Eichen-Butte to anyone over middle-school age — immediately herded Jack into the rest of the group, so she could introduce the cave guide and make other announcements. Despite her name and reputation, Mrs. Icky-Butt was positively bubbling. She even smiled. Jack was sure he had never seen his teacher smile. *It must be the ocean air.*

"We would like to thank the nice folks at Winnacutlet State Park for their assistance in arranging this and guiding us through this treacherous terrain." She nodded at the cave guide. "In the event of lightning, we will return to the bus immediately." Without another word, she jaunted off eagerly in the direction of the cave. Everyone, including the guide, was caught by surprise and dashed to catch up.

Once in the cave, Jack had expected bugs, bats and cave slime but saw only one spider near the entrance. Farther in, there was nothing creepy. In fact, it was not until they had been walking several minutes that the walls finally began to transform from dirty bedrock to something more interesting.

This far down, the cave walls glistened from the light of a handful of electric lanterns carried by the class. The cave guide occasionally shined a spotlight on areas of particular interest, and Mrs. Icky-Butt's descriptions resounded in shrill echoes throughout the cavern. "Stalagmites are the spiny and stubby deposits on the floor of the cave," she said. Her penetrating voice left Jack half-certain one of the thicker stalactites would break loose solely from the pitch of her voice and squish him. He would die less than a minute after having learned what the word "stalactite" even meant.

He gave a cagey glance at the cave's ceiling.

Unbidden, the words from the text message flashed through his mind. *In the cave with your friends, as the words "spiny and stubby" are spoken, you must turn left.*

At the back of the class, nobody took notice of Jack's sudden standstill. They continued to follow the two adults, disappearing around a bend in the cave.

Jack's hair stood on end.

How had Chase known Icky-Butt would say those exact words? They had different teachers, and Icky-Butt was not following any kind of script. Jack suddenly realized there was no reason to believe Chase had sent the messages at all. In fact, Jack was now convinced it could not have been him, but then who? And how could anyone have known Icky-Butt would say those exact words and when?

Do not follow them. Turn left. Follow the pull. He pictured the strange text message in his mind.

To his left, at the base of the cave wall, was a small opening. It was hardly visible. Jack was unsure if he would even fit. A faint, purple glow seeped from the hole—but only indirectly, from the corners of his eyes.

Follow the pull, the message had said. As he thought about it, there was a gentle tug against him. He definitely felt it—a soft, insistent pull drawing him, bidding him to follow.

He made his decision, took one last glimpse around, and decided to follow it. He scrunched himself down and squeezed in headfirst. The tunnel was not much bigger than Jack. He had to shimmy most of the way through, unable to walk or even crawl. Cold, damp and slimy, the tunnel walls were coated with ooze. He was grateful he could see little in the dim glow. The tunnel sloped farther into the ground.

After what seemed an hour, but was probably only minutes, the faint purple glow bloomed in size. Jack's hand felt an opening.

He worked his body from the tunnel into a cavern. Every sound echoed off the walls. He saw the hollow den clearly, but had no idea why. It should have been black as pitch this far beneath the ground. The faint purple glow suffused everything—not bright, but enough for him to see.

At the center of the cave was a small pool of water, clear and perfectly still. A constant drip echoed rhythmically, unseen in the stillness. In the middle was the source of the curious purple glow. Jack waded to it and spotted a rock, slightly smaller than a baseball— the source of the unnatural glow that filled the cavern. The driving, pulling sensation was stronger now, unrelenting.

He stooped to pick up the stone. His eyes grew wide as he brought it level with his nose. It began pulsing, a bright purple light. No sooner had he stood fully than a strange sensation thundered through him. His legs turned to jelly. His mind reeled.

Everything went black.

Chapter Three
Extraordinarily Ordinary

———

Jack awoke in the middle of that shallow pool, clutching the strange rock tightly in his fist. With no idea how long he had been unconscious, he knew he had better get back to the rest of the class—and fast. He was dripping wet, his clothes surely a mess.

He clambered his way back up through the tunnel, out the other side, and popped his head out as the last of the class passed on their way from the cave. He fell in with them, trying his best to look normal, certain someone would notice his wet and muddy clothes. Nobody mentioned them.

Taking his seat at the back of the bus, he found his loose-fitting jeans and brown cargo-style coat spotless. He held the rock to his face and studied it. Other than being so light in weight, there was nothing special about it. The strange spectral glow was gone. It was little more than an ordinary chunk of stone.

Chapter Four

A Sign of the Times

H ey, did you text me this morning? A little after nine?" Jack stopped walking suddenly and stared at Chase. He had deliberately waited until the two were almost halfway home from school before bringing up the subject. The last thing he wanted was for some other kid to overhear this particular conversation.

"Are you kidding me? I was in class."

Jack was expecting that. The more he thought about it, he knew it could not have been Chase. There simply was no logical explanation for it.

"Well, you're not going to believe this, but …" He stopped talking and focused past Chase, who spun around to see what had caught Jack's attention. It was a house that had been converted to a boutique.

"What?" Chase asked.

They had passed that store hundreds of times, every day on the way to and from school. It was the same decaying, little white house it always was—dingy, with rotting cedar panels and a sagging roof. A neon sign blinked in the window with pink cursive letters. "Madame Puffin—Fortuneteller," it said, the same as always. Jack had spotted a piece of paper taped to the glass-paned door. That was new. He could not explain why it grabbed his attention, but it did.

"Oh. That sign." Jack waved loosely at the fortune-teller's shop and walked a few paces until he could read the writing.

Free Fortunes Today
8 people

"So?"

With the peculiarity of his experience in the caves that morning, the idea somehow felt right. Jack angled toward the front steps. "Come on. We're getting a free fortune."

Chapter Five
Of Fortunes and Puffins

M adame Puffin, esteemed member of the Witch Associates Council, inched back from the door. She had to scurry all the way into the back room to avoid being caught. The door clanged open minutes after she had taped up the sign.

Two twelve-year-old boys clomped in, arguing mildly in the foyer. It was most infuriating. Not because they were bickering in her store, but because they were not bickering loudly enough. She could barely hear a word they said.

The tall one—scrawny with dark, curly hair—wore preppy clothes fit to perfection. Smaller by an inch or two, the little one was far more relaxed and scrappy. He ran his hand through bushy hair. Jack. Madame Puffin knew him well, though he did not know her. She had to smile as the boy listened patiently to his friend's objections.

"… nothing is free—your money vanishing—that's the only magic you'll see." The tall one finished with a mock spell, fingers wiggling up into the air.

"Hell-oooo." Her singsong voice startled the two boys, so she gave them a slight bow. "I'm Madame Puffin, oh."

Jack turned to face her. "Hi. Um, the sign says you'll give eight

free fortunes today?" Despite his heavy clothes, he was beet-red from cold.

"Oh, dear. Is that how it appears? Oh no, my dear. It says 'B People,' I fear. For does your name—either—begin with a B, or neither?"

The two boys glanced at each other, but Jack worked out her

question first. "Um. I'm a Boomer … er, well, my name is Jack Boomershine."

"Wonderful, young man. Then we shall proceed. Your fortune today I shall gladly read. Oh heavens, one moment—nix it. I must take down that sign and fix it." She shuffled to the front door and removed the sign from beneath the curtain, setting it down absently with no intention of ever using it again. It had served its purpose.

Chase let out a sigh. Jack gave him a blustery look and turned back toward her.

"Well, well, I'm so sorry. Back again," she said, walking back to the pair. "Please, please, shall we begin?"

"Sure." Jack smiled.

"That would be wonderful," Chase said with no trace of sincerity. Madame Puffin did not know him as well as Jack, but she knew enough to know he had never been good at holding sarcasm.

She stood in place, staring at them, while Jack nervously looked about the store. She needed no magic to read his thoughts. She had always found Jack an easy study. Aside from that, she had known him his whole life. The boy would not remember it now, but Madame Puffin's face was the first he had ever seen in his life.

Chapter Six
From Within Strength Comes

———

J ack looked about nervously.

The shop was not unlike an old-time ice cream parlor with large windows that would let the sun shine in—if Brighton only had some. It had window seats with burgundy cushions, green and white striped curtains, a shiny black and white tiled floor, and a long-necked ceiling fan turning so slowly it could not possibly have been moving much of anything.

Unlike in an ice cream parlor, there were no tables or chairs. Jack turned to look at the fortune teller, who said nothing more.

Her dark hair was so loosely curled that it spiraled away from her head in waves. Orchids in red, pink and yellow blanketed her muumuu, which flowed in baggy ripples that trailed behind, tracing each change in direction as she moved.

Jack thought she might want them to sit down the way they do in the movies—some place with a crystal ball. He spotted only the window seats.

Madame Puffin continued to stare at the two, but then finally turned to Jack. "Ah, poor Jack, don't pretend. May I ask the name of your friend?" Her voice was pitched and fluty.

"Oh. I'm sorry. This is Chase, Chase Lucre."

"Pleased to meet you," Chase said under his breath.

Her face animated. "Well, yes. So nice to meet you, too. And a hearty welcome to both of you. Well then, perhaps we should proceed."

She took Jack by the hands and fixed her eyes on his. "Oh, and no. A crystal ball we don't need. Necessary? They aren't really. Just you. That's all we really need, silly."

Jack glanced at Chase's eyes and imagined him saying the same thing he had when the boys had seen a woman cradling a cured ham in a pink baby blanket. "She's a fruitcake. A nutcase." His eyes had looked the same.

"Ok, first a little background. Doom or fine …" Madame Puffin's eyes went distant for a moment. "You are Jack … Jack … you are Jack Boomershine."

"He might have mentioned that," Chase said. Jack gave him another burning look, at which Chase shrugged. Madame Puffin seemed not to notice.

She tugged on Jack's ears, stuck out her tongue and blew a raspberry in his face. Suddenly her eyes glistened with clarity, blue and striking. She inhaled sharply and said, "Your life, as you have always known it, is about to change."

A chill ran up Jack's spine.

She made a few more rude sounds with her tongue, pinched Jack's nose and then continued. "From this day, for you, things will never be any less than strange. Stand at the edge of a large cliff, you do. Looking down, very soon, the time for change will come for you. It will be change that is both very good and very bad, and I'm afraid I can tell you neither the hard nor the glad. But it would not matter, for I can change neither." She gave a sad shake of her head. "Of course, nor can you either."

Jack nodded thoughtfully. Chase scowled thoughtlessly.

The old fortune-teller continued. "You build things replete with electronics, eager to discover technology. Friends you treat with magic tricks, and fool others with mere psychology. Though gratifying, but never satisfying, perhaps it is some hole in you, you seek to fill. Though pacifying, it's magnifying this need within you still. For all the mock-magic you employ, there is so much more than pretend. You might be wise to find real arts to deploy, for others on you depend. Forget not that from within strength comes, and matter not how much you find fear numbs. The time to be strong is upon you, and regardless of the weight put on you, you are strong."

Her voice hit the lowest, most whispery note it could register as she added, "And it is always from within strength comes."

Chapter Seven
A Pesky Delay

T he moment she stopped speaking, the air was sucked from the room—and out of Madame Puffin besides. She collapsed wearily as Jack stumbled forward to support her. A breeze blew past, wind poured away from them. Jack's ears popped. He worked his mouth open and closed a few times and noticed Chase doing the same.

Chase scanned the room, evidently trying to find the source of the mysterious pressure drop. He rubbed his jaw, staring suspiciously at the ceiling fan, which may well have been moving slower than before, were that possible.

It took Madame Puffin a minute to compose herself and regain her footing. Her voice cracked as she said, "Ah, we are done. Was it any fun?"

Jack was shocked. "You mean you don't know?"

"Remember I cannot all that you begot in the midst of the dance." She inclined her head sheepishly. "I am quite unaware while in a trance."

"Ummm. I didn't understand most of it." He rubbed his nose where she had tweaked it and eyed the floor as if it were truly fascinating.

"That's ok, and normal, too." She lowered her voice to a hush. "When most you need it, perhaps it will come to you."

She gave a little wink and brightened. "Let me see, young man, let me see. In the back, I may have a spot of help for you—a key."

The odd fortune-teller padded off to the back room where, a moment later, drawers opened and shut, a door slammed, cardstock riffled and glass broke.

Poof!

A puff of smoke and a small flash of light came from above them. Jack nearly collapsed to the floor in surprise—convinced that Puffin had done something, but unsure what. A piece of vellum fluttered down from above, gliding to rest at his feet.

He picked it up—an aged vellum paper, curled at the ends like a scroll. Flowing letters arced gracefully across it.

"Our arrival shortly. Chance not his departure." Chase read it aloud, pressed over Jack's shoulder. It was signed with a simple P.

Jack reread it more than once, and gazed in the direction of the back room as more strange sounds issued from it. Without so much as a glance or a nod at each other, the boys rushed out the door.

Chapter Eight
Chase's Place

—

S he's a nutcase." Chase stormed a few more paces before adding, "And you are, too."

"Me? How am I a nutcase?"

"You fell for it. Didn't you?"

Jack said nothing in reply.

The two had run for several minutes after leaving the little shop. They probably would not have, but Madame Puffin and two other people—one, an older man with a thick British accent—chased them down the block a little before falling behind.

A cold, light drizzle had started. Although it was not much, Jack was sodden from head to toe. Breath steamed in foggy puffs before them.

"You were running as fast as I was."

"I don't mean that, stupid. I mean you believed her. That whole line about standing on a cliff and all that."

"Oh. How did she know all the stuff about me, anyway?"

"And what was with that rhyming thing?" Chase asked. "That was driving me crazy."

"I thought it was pretty amazing. How do you think she comes up with all those rhymes without even trying?"

"She probably gave you the same fortune she gave the last fifty people. By now, she's got them all worked out."

There was no way she had given that fortune to anyone else. Magic tricks, psychological tricks, building electronic things—Jack knew that was all him.

As it was getting dark, they arrived at Chase's house. After a quick hello to his parents, they went up to his room. Chase's parents offered to take them out for ice cream, but neither of them had wanted to go back out. Cold and edgy, all Jack wanted was a blanket.

Chapter Nine
Rock and Roll

———

I'm telling you, Puffin was going to try to sell you something."
Chase was sprawled belly-down across the blue blanket on his
bed. His head was propped up—arms on elbows—and his feet
zoomed anxiously through the air behind him in some complex sign
language.

"Yeah." Jack was half-listening.

When he had called his parents to check in and remind them that
he was sleeping at Chase's, his dad had been unusually somber. He
had said that tomorrow when Jack got home they would "have to
discuss something."

That was not like him. Jack could not stop thinking he was in
trouble but had no idea why.

Chase continued his rant. "… how they work. They get you all
worked up about some horrific future they've cooked up, and get you
to buy things to make it better."

"Yeah."

"An enchanted rooster's feather, frog's legs, eye of newt. I mean
it's all over the news."

Jack looked up from his thoughts. "That stuff's not in the news.
And besides, you're the only kid I know who follows the news."

"Well, we all should."

"You're the only kid I know who reads the financial papers."

"It's fun," Chase said, his voice suddenly hollow.

"Seventh graders don't read *The Economist*. Our parents don't even read *The Economist*. Only old guys in suits do." He knew he was being harsh, but there was only so much criticism a guy could take before he blew, and he had heard enough about his decision to go into that store.

Jack leaned back in the desk chair absently holding the rock in his hands. The chair squealed. It had to be a hundred years old—a cast-iron office chair on wheels Chase's parents had gotten from some yard sale, or rescued dumpster-diving. It weighed a million pounds.

Chase was being unreasonable. Besides, he was odd. He constantly read every bit of financial news he could get his hands on, determined to be a corporate banker before he was twenty.

It would have been one thing if Chase's parents had driven him to it, but his parents were two of the most laid-back, down-to-earth people Jack knew.

Posters around Chase's room were of the Chair of the Federal Reserve, the Secretary of the United States Treasury Department, and one signed by a former President.

Who does that? Jack wondered.

Unlike that of any other kid they knew, Chase's room was stark white, with wood paneling he had picked out himself—a conference room with a bed.

Jack had to admit they were more alike than not, though. Jack had his own peculiarities, and both boys were virtual outcasts at school for the things they enjoyed, things nobody else understood. Chase would never poke fun at Jack for what lay scattered about his room, and Jack would not normally jab at Chase either, but it had been a long day.

He stared at the rock in his hands, rolling it around and around. *Strange how light it is.*

Finished stewing, Chase returned to the subject. "And that parchment-out-of-the-air thing was a cheap trick."

"Snap!" Jack almost yelled it.

"It was, though."

Focused on the rock, Jack said, "No, I totally forgot to tell you about the class trip this morning."

"So? Our class went on that two days ago."

"No, really. I can't believe I forgot to tell you. You've got to hear this. I started to tell you before we went into that shop, and I guess I forgot after."

He told the story of how he had found the stone and the messages that preceded it. Jack studied the rock but kept looking to Chase for his reaction.

"Ok. That's weird. I never sent you any text messages. You know I can't touch a phone in class."

"Yeah, I didn't really think it was you. Well, at least not after everything that happened in the cave." Jack held up the rock for Chase to see. "There's something weird about this thing."

Chase popped up. "Let me see it."

Jack held it out, about to hand it over.

Boom!

A bright flash of purple light and thick smoke erupted from the rock in Jack's hand.

Chapter Ten

Persisting Pursuit Perception

As the rock exploded, Chase fell back on his heels, landing on his haunches.

Jack dropped the stone.

Through the clearing purple smoke, a gaping hole materialized in the floor. The acrid smell of burning wood floated, heavy in the air.

"Oh, crap. My parents are going to kill me."

Jack watched the door, ready for Chase's parents to burst in. Nobody did.

After a few moments of silence with the boys glaring gravely at the door, Chase went to see if his family had heard anything. Seconds later, he came back. "They must have gone out for ice cream without us. Nobody's home."

"You are so lucky."

Neither of them went anywhere near the rock, which had fallen to the floor and rolled a little in the direction of the desk, unharmed.

Jack took the desk chair again, which had escaped damage. It was built like a tank. He put his head down. "No way."

"It's fine," Chase said, "but I'm not sure what happens when Mom and Dad come home."

"No. It's not that. I just thought of something." Jack focused on the floor, nervously smoothing back the hair on the side of his head.

"Again?"

"That lady. I've seen her before."

"Who?"

"Madame Puffin."

"Well, of course you have. We walk that way every day." Chase smirked.

"No. I mean, I've seen her before. Everywhere. A lot. I've seen her at the store, at the movies, at restaurants. And every time I've caught her looking at me."

"No way."

"I mean, I knew when we first went into her shop she looked familiar, and I was trying to remember from where. But now that I think about it, where *haven't* I seen her?"

"Weird," Chase said, his face unconvinced.

Certain Chase thought he was being melodramatic, Jack realized that maybe he was. Brighton was not that big. Surely if you paid attention, you would see the same people again and again. *Besides, why would she have been following me?*

Checking for any residual heat or embers first, the boys hid the hole in the floor with a pile of spare blankets and put a fan in the window. It was a little cold, but they had to get the rank smell of burning timbers out of the room.

Adjusting the fan in the window casement, Chase noticed something out the window and wordlessly nodded at Jack to see.

Two eyes, glowing golden yellow in the night, glared directly at them. As the boys backed away from the window, the bird took flight and flew a sweeping arc across the back yard, into the sky.

"Must have been a raven or an owl or something," Chase said.

Jack was not so sure.

Chapter Eleven
Your Parents Are Positively Glowing

The next day, Jack arrived home after grudgingly retrieving the stone from the floor beneath Chase's desk. At first, he touched it carefully—afraid at any moment it would explode in a flash of purple light and smoke. Luckily, nothing happened. What else could he do? There was no way Chase would have gone near it, and Jack did not want to leave it there after everything he had gone through to get it in the first place.

Lost in thought, he felt uneasy about the events of the day before. He seemed stuck in the middle of something. For the first time in his life, it was something he could not explain. Somehow, it felt big. It felt dangerous.

"Son." His dad called from the formal living room—the one room in the house where nobody ever went, the room where air itself had to get approval before entering. Jack could not help thinking how much better the room would be with a pool table.

As he walked in, his parents were sitting stiffly on the couch, his mother on the armrest at his father's side.

"There is a matter we must discuss," his father said. "Please sit down."

This was not like his parents. With the slight nod his father gave, Jack noticed one other peculiar thing. A very light, almost imperceptible, green glow clung to his parents in wisps, as if they had stepped out of a green fog.

He sat down, as directed, into an overstuffed armchair across from them—certain he was in trouble for something but with no idea for what.

"Yesterday, we received some distressing news." His father never talked like that. Mom sat there with what looked like a forced smile across her face. She had not said a word. That was not like her, either. Whatever Jack had done, it must have been really, really bad.

"We received the results from a laboratory test," Dad said. "A test that shows you are not our son."

Chapter Twelve

A Minor Case of Cankrot

What?" Jack's mouth fell open, but nothing would come out.

"You heard me, son." The tone was cold, like Jack had broken a window playing baseball—as if he had been harboring the secret of not being their son for years, and it was about time he had gotten around to telling them the truth.

"It's amazing, I know. It seems you were switched at birth with another boy." Dad sat stock-still. Mom gave a slightly larger, quirky smile but said nothing.

"What?"

"Your mom and I are beside ourselves. It's horrible." Neither face reflected, in the slightest, the anxiety in those words. If anything, Dad was stern while Mom seemed daft. An absurd wax grimace was pressed onto her lips, pretending to be a smile.

There was still that greenish aura, making them look like glow-in-the-dark Walter and Carly Anne Homemaker dolls.

None of this made any sense.

"You mean …"

"Yes. You are not our son. Your real name is actually Caitiff Cankrot Junior, born of Caitiff and Oleagina Cankrot."

Jack's head was spinning. "Kee-tiff?"

"Yes. He sometimes goes by Kee."

He tried mumbling the other name to himself. "Olee … Olee?"

"O-lee-adge-in-ah," Dad said, sounding it out. "Yes. She goes by Gina."

Jack got so lightheaded he thought he might pass out. For a split second, the green radiance faded. As it flickered, the expression on his parents' faces turned real. Tortured sadness spread across them both—especially Mom, who struggled visibly.

The moment passed as quickly as it had come. The green glow strengthened. Their faces returned to the dysfunctional way they had been, marked smiles and all. The doorbell rang. The foul aura that radiated from them now was brighter than ever, far brighter than when he had first come into the room.

In unison, his parents hopped up from the couch and, with matching strides, walked to the door.

"Ah." His father's voice came from the foyer, still without a word from Mom. "Good morning, Mr. and Mrs. Cankrot. I see you have come to collect your son."

"Ah yes, Mr. Boomershine, or may I call you Walter? Ever so good to see you again. And Carly, of course." The man's voice was thin and reedy, an accent of British English.

It occurred to Jack that it was the second time in two days that he had heard a British accent. The other was the man behind Madame Puffin as the boys ran from the store. That one seemed to have a deeper, throatier voice. Other than those in movies, though, Jack had never heard one before yesterday. There had to be a connection. This had to have something to do with Puffin.

Jack sat fixed in his armchair, around the corner from the foyer, listening.

"I trust you have had a chance to explain?" It was a woman's oily voice, thick with the same accent.

"Yes. Yes. As a matter of fact, that was just what we were discussing."

"Stupendous," the man said with a slithery hiss that made Jack shudder.

"If you will, Mr. and Mrs. Cankrot, this way please." Jack's father led them into the living room. The green haze was now so thick it nearly obscured his parents' faces. Even more alarming was that the glow now had a distinct pulse.

Chapter Thirteen
A Reasonable Request

Ah, there's the boy." The man straightened when he saw Jack. He was bony and a bit shorter than Jack's parents. Straight and greasy, his hair was black as coal. His beard line hinted that he constantly needed a shave. Wet patches beneath the arms of his white, though yellowing, button-down shirt were obvious. The word "sour" immediately sprang to Jack's mind.

"Ah. Our little Kee. Kee junior." The woman sang the words, as if talking to an infant. Jack expected her to prattle on with goos and gahs.

She was a finger shorter than the man, who had relaxed into a slump he seemed well acquainted with. Like him, she had straight, black, oily hair, though longer. She was rounder in the face, but the bridge of her nose was large and lumpy and had a way of commanding attention. Her eyes lit at Jack, as if she were being presented an exotic thrill.

Jack had the absurd feeling that these people were somehow controlling his parents. He knew the idea of it was crazy and had no idea how they might be pulling it off, but somehow he could feel it. He knew he was right. The green, pulsing glow around his parents

added to his certainty.

The woman's voice screeched a little too loudly as she extended her arms and said, "Come to me, my son."

Jack ran a hand through his hair. Though repulsed, he suddenly felt that he knew what he had to do. Play along.

At that moment, he would not have been able to explain how he knew. It just came to him. These were not his parents. He knew that. He had the feeling his real parents were trapped—they could do nothing. These people, the Cankrots, were behind his parents' strange behavior, somehow—maybe even the source of the green glow. Whoever these people were, they had power—power enough to be able to control his parents.

If he fought them on this, he had a feeling they could turn that power on him. In fact, he wondered why they had not done exactly that.

If he could not win a fight with them, there was only one thing left.

He forced a smile to his face, much like those his parents wore, and stepped forward into this strange woman's arms. "Mommy," he said, feeling ridiculous.

After a moment, he turned and ran into the man's arms. "Daddy."

The man was less amenable to the hug, and both he and Jack kept it blessedly brief. Jack found in that brusque hug that the man was indeed sour in more than just manner.

"Ah, stupendous. Absolutely stupendous," the wiry man said. "So you will come with us?" Jack's parents stood mutely by, smiling those dotty smiles.

"Of course, of course." Jack responded with over-exuberance to match. "Could I, er … Could I have some time to gather my things?" He took a breath. It was now or never. "And say goodbye to a few friends?"

Kee, the wiry man, tightened his brow in confusion. He had not expected that, but the woman, Gina, quickly filled the silence. "Absolutely, little Kee."

Her face grew stern in a quick shot to the man and then expanded in false generosity as she turned again to Jack. "An absolutely reasonable request," she said with the singsong voice.

"Stupendous. I could be ready for you by," he glanced at his watch, "shall we say two?" That would give him four hours.

He got them to agree, though both seemed more than a little confused how he had done it, and hustled them out the door amid a number of uncomfortable and equally phony goodbyes.

Chapter Fourteen
Glow Detector

T he door clicked shut behind the Cankrots.

The house was silent.

Jack turned to his parents, throbbing with that steady green glow. They stared blankly at him and blinked. They smiled those dull smiles.

Jack got the willies.

He turned up the stairs, taking the rock from his pocket. It bumped off his backpack and fell to the ground, rolling back along the floor. He bent to pick it up and realized the green aura around his parents was gone. As his fingers touched the stone, the glimmer resumed.

By touching and letting go a few times, he confirmed that the glow never really went away. The rock allowed him to see what could not be seen.

With a growing hollow in his gut, he ran up the stairs.

Chapter Fifteen

Should Have Used the Jetpack

J ack sat on his bed and let out a heavy sigh.

Four hours. What can I possibly do in four hours?

For a moment, he felt closed in, stuck. He had no options, nothing at all he could do. He wanted to run from the house and the glowing green parents it held. He wanted to throw this stupid rock into the ocean, from where it had probably come in the first place. He wanted to run from Puffin and the Cankrots.

They were watching the house, though. He knew they would be. There was no way he could just leave. He tried to think through the situation.

These people were going to take him. To where and why, he did not know.

He surveyed his room, filled with gizmos and gadgets, half-worked doodads—as his mom had always called them—and drawings for still more. His laboratory.

He was an inventor, or he would be one day.

One such invention sat on the corner of his desk—a console for controlling things in his room, like the blinds and the ceiling fan. Another of his creations was propped up beside the console—an ultra-efficient battery pack he was working on to be the main source of power for his jetpack. The jetpack itself was lying against the wall by the closet, only slightly damaged from his mishap two nights before. Neither was finished, but they were close. Always close.

He realized how many were close but not quite done. With the inventions he had completed, he wowed his friends. They were amazed at what he could do with whatever spare parts he found lying around. From a radio or broken-down old cell phone, he could salvage pieces to make a control board for a robot and a remote-control relay. Between his inventions and his love of magic tricks, particularly sleight of hand, he amazed his friends.

While Jack knew that Chase enjoyed the magic tricks, he also knew that in his inventions, Chase saw their future. He knew Chase was convinced that when they were older, Jack would do the inventing, and Chase would manage the banking. He talked of business plans, marketing and getting investors as if it were another piece of him—which in a way it was.

As seriously as Jack took his inventions, Chase took his finance. He read about banking and high corporate deals in stock market magazines and Wall Street newspapers as Jack would read science and technology magazines.

As Jack peered over the room, he just felt sad.

He kicked the homemade contraption closest to his feet, a fragile crane-like machine he had not worked on in months. It collapsed in a heap. Servos and gears scattered in pieces across the floor.

He held the strange rock tightly in his hand. It had all started with the rock.

Your life, as you have always known it, is about to change. Puffin's giggly voice hummed through his head.

It was eerie how quickly that fortune had come true. In truth, she had played a part in it, though. Hadn't she?

He could not imagine why she had done any of this. Or why she had sent those two to get him. That had to be a connection. He had never met anyone with a British accent in his life, and in two days, he had met three. One of them was with Puffin. That is, if you counted someone chasing you as meeting them. It was a bit of a stretch, but he counted it anyway.

The correct answer is usually the simplest, his father would say when he was not glowing green. Occam's Razor, he called it.

There was a connection. There had to be.

He was getting nowhere with this. He had to do something and soon. The appointed hour was drawing closer.

He scanned the room again.

All of his inventions and half-finished devices were scattered about. None of them could help him now when he needed them most. He hefted the rock in his hand and squeezed.

A thought popped into his head. *Or can they?*

Maybe his inventions were exactly what he needed.

Chapter Sixteen
Nobody Can Be Invisible

_____

J ack had not left his room. He handled the communication through text messages on his cell. If the Cankrots were listening somehow, they would never know what he had in mind. All the same, if they were invisible and looking over his shoulder, he was in trouble.

He shook his head at the thought. Nobody can be invisible.

He hit "Send" on the last message:

```
right, but dont untie it anywhr near here
```

After a short wait, the reply came.

Jack smiled.

Chapter Seventeen
Bodged Scrap

G ina walked up to Kee, who was standing in the middle of the street—heedless of cars—in front of the Boomershine house. They were both invisible and quite immune to cars in their present state.

"Anything?" he asked.

"No," she said. "That little girl is just driving the robot up the pavement. Back to her own house, I presume. You?"

"Nah. Two more, including that one." He nodded in the direction of the house, where Jack stood smiling broadly in the doorway, animatedly talking to some other little kid Kee did not recognize.

Jack ducked back inside, leaving the other child standing at the door. It had been the same routine the last eight or ten times. Kee had lost count.

"Same thing." He ruffled, reflexively looking at his watch, which—being invisible—he could not see. "I think he's saying his goodbyes and giving away his most precious tokens."

Jack came back out with a large trunk on a dolly. The dolly seemed to have a hydraulic mechanism built in. As he pushed a button on a small handheld remote, the trunk lowered to the ground. Another button press and the lid slid open with a loud click and a hydraulic hum. The new kid laughed with delight.

"Where does he get this stuff?" Kee asked. Gina stood mum.

Jack reached down into the trunk, lifting various items one at a time—several large and a few small—and briefly explained the function of each. He handed the controller to the other boy and seemed to provide a few details about how to use that as well. The other boy pushed a button, and the lid mechanically slid shut.

Jack gave one last deep wave and a smile and went back inside.

The other boy stood for a moment examining the remote, trying to remember how to use all the buttons. He noticed his shoe was untied and stooped to tie it. Once he got back up, he began pushing buttons until the dolly sprang to life and surged forward down the sidewalk.

"Think I should follow him?"

"Nah. He's going to be giving that bodged scrap away for the next two hours."

He looked around and, in the general direction of where the invisible Gina ought to be, Kee asked, "Say, you up for a sandwich?"

Chapter Eighteen
Pop Goes the Weasel

J ack felt like he was folded into a box of crackers, baking in the sun. His ribs were throbbing from his recent attempt at merging with a tree at high speed. Three jarring bumps did not help, but at least they were easier on his ailing sides than his tailbone. He heard a door slam and a whistled round of "Pop Goes the Weasel" through the walls of his hiding spot, to which he could only shake his head. At the right spot in the song, the lid opened to Chase's beaming face, and Jack jumped up.

"Thanks. It was getting hot in there." He wiped his brow and took a few deep breaths. "Think anyone followed you?"

"I don't think so, but I didn't see anyone at your house, either."

"Me either, but I think they were watching. If not, then at least I did a little room cleaning. Mom's been on me to do that for a while."

"So how'd you do it?"

"Ah. Piece of cake. I went out the dog door at the house and into this fake side." Jack pushed a latch on the side of the trunk, and it swung in.

Chase grinned. "But where did all the stuff go?"

"You mean this stuff?" He pressed another button, and the bigger items in the trunk reappeared, unfolding from the bottom and sides like a pop-up book. "The small stuff I pushed back into the dog door."

"Whoa. That's cool. I never would have figured that out."

"Thanks."

"Now if only you'd use that mind for good."

Jack chuckled. "Look, I don't know how much time we have. Let's get up to your room."

Chapter Nineteen
Safe Haven

———

You think it's safe here?" Chase plopped on his bed while Jack took the desk chair—their usual positions. Each boy spent as much time in the other's room as he did in his own.

"I dunno." Jack took the rock from his pocket, absently kneading it. "Maybe not. They might have followed us here last night even. Hard to say."

Chase's eyes lit at the sight of the stone. "Hey, no blowing any more holes in my floor. I might not have any floor left. Anyway, I doubt they followed us. We left them in the dust."

"I don't know, Chase." He leaned back in the chair. "These people can do weird things." He launched into the story of how he found his parents when he came home and what happened with the Cankrots. "I need to figure out what to do next. I think I've got till two. Sooner or later, they're going to come looking for me again. And what do I do about my parents' ... well, my parents' greenishness?"

Chase was uncharacteristically silent, thinking through Jack's words. "What have you gotten mixed up in?"

"Or maybe it's this thing they're looking for." He held up the rock.

Three bright flashes flooded the room with light.

With each came a person.

Chapter Twenty
My Room Really Is Not That Big

J ack quickly stuffed the rock back into his pocket.

Screaming, yelling and chaos filled Chase's small bedroom. Madame Puffin was among the three, but Jack did not recognize the other two.

The boys jumped up, trying to get to the door amid the commotion, but Madame Puffin blocked the way.

An older man yelled, "Stop!" freezing everyone in place. Jack finally recognized him—when Madame Puffin had chased them down the street the night before, he was the one bringing up the rear.

The third person, a young girl, was about the same age as the boys. She had curly, springy, blonde hair and was taller than Jack and Chase. For some reason, the rhinestone peace symbol emblazoned on her purple shirt struck Jack as ironic.

The room fell silent. Jack stared at the older man, who cleared his throat and tugged in umbrage at the hem of his vest, straightening it. It was a dusty three-piece, woolen suit, about forty years out of date. He looked every bit a crazy old man—white hair strewn and sticking out at the sides, skin lined with age, rumpled cheeks, and a fiery red, blistered nose poked well past the front of his face.

He straightened his short frame and took them all in. "Very

good." It was that British accent again, his voice deep and resonant.

"I believe we can discuss this matter equitably." By his tone, he brooked no doubt. "But first, perhaps we should have some introductions all around. Shall we?"

Silence.

"Ah. In that case, I shall begin. My name is Master Pescipalius Dorfnutter, senior member of the British Council of Wizards, and acting superintendent of the Board of Trustees of said council." He scanned the room and took a breath, rolling his eyes slightly. "Certain people may insist—to my utter bafflement—on calling me Pesky, to which I am not inclined to offense."

He gave a slight, bureaucratic nod to Madame Puffin, indicating he had finished.

She softly cleared her throat and began without taking a breath. "Madame Toulouse Beatrice Puffin," she said, with a small regal motion toward herself and no accent. "We have already met, you'll remember." She gave a curt nod to the boys. "Of the aforesaid council, I too am a senior member. Of the Board of Prophecy sitting on that council, the appointed Senior Chair. And of the Witch Associates Council, I am also a member extraordinaire."

At Puffin's last word, Chase let out a small, nervous giggle while everyone else in the room turned to the third person who had arrived in a flash of light and smoke—the young girl. She must not have expected anyone to talk to her, because the look that came across her face was one of perfect surprise.

"Um. Well, I'm Vidalia. Vidalia Dorfnutter. Pescipalius' daughter." Her accent was thicker and not nearly so refined as her father's. From the first look on her face, Jack assumed she would be shy, but if she was, she covered it well. Her words were strong and clear and gave no indication she was nervous. She turned to Jack, her sandy blonde hair coiled and bobbed slightly at the motion.

"And I'm Jack Boomershine," he said, glancing around the room once, "inventor." It seemed to be in keeping with the other introductions.

All eyes in the room moved to Jack's friend. "Uh, Chase. Chase Lucre, and this is my room." He gave a cheery wave. Jack felt that was a little much, considering the circumstances.

"Excellent," the man named Pescipalius said. His voice boomed in the small room. "Now with that out of the way, let me begin by saying we are not here to hurt you. In all actuality, Mr. Boomershine, we are here to help and protect you."

"Yeah, right. Like you protected my parents?"

Pescipalius and Madame Puffin exchanged a baffled glance, before Madame Puffin asked, "What was that, Jack?"

"My parents. You turned them into green robots."

At the perplexed stare that came across Puffin's face, Jack added, "Well, not you, exactly, but those other people you sent."

Pescipalius asked him to start from the beginning.

Jack explained the events that had happened from the moment he came home — his parents' discussion of the lab results and the sudden appearance of the Cankrots to take him away. "I know those people are not my parents," he said, wanting to say more but not sure what.

Pescipalius straightened. "Vidalia."

"Yes, Daddy?"

"Do you remember the Boomershine house and how to get there?" He gave a quick, guilt-ridden eye toward Jack.

"Of course."

"Do you think you can steal a glimpse without disclosing your whereabouts?"

"I'm certain I can."

"Excellent, then please do so."

An eager smile, another flash, and she was gone.

Chapter Twenty-One
A Firestorm or Something

N obody said anything for several minutes. Madame Puffin looked peeved by the turn of events, but Jack wondered if that was how she looked when uneasy.

"*Mister* Boomershine." Despite his refined accent, Jack thought Pescipalius sounded like a gym teacher saying his name that way. "First, I must tell you that we did not send those people, but we think we know who did."

"Ok then, who?"

"I will come to that, I assure you. For now, I simply wanted to point out that I came because Madame Puffin was concerned about you." Pesky gestured lightly in her direction. "And I must admit, having heard of this latest discovery, I now share her gravest apprehensions. You mentioned your parents as 'green robots,' as I recall." It was not exactly a question.

Madame Puffin shot Jack a curious glance. "Yes, what did you mean by that?"

"Er, well, my parents have a ... well, it's kind of a glow. And it's green."

"And you can see it?"

"Yes. Well, sort of." He pulled the rock from his pocket. "Every time I'm holding this, I can." In his mind, he kicked himself. He had not meant to tell them about the rock.

Their eyes widened in surprise. Madame Puffin's jaw actually dropped open, before she seemed to realize the impropriety and quickly shut it.

"Every time I let go of it, the glow disappears."

Everyone in the room stared in silence at the stone in Jack's palm, as if it would flash neon or start dancing. It did neither. Even Chase stared in wonder at it, but Jack was pretty sure he was just trying to understand what the big deal was.

"Great gads and flying zooks, m'boy!" Pesky yelled louder than he needed to. With a lurch, Jack almost dropped the stone.

"Bea? Do you think … ?"

"Yes. Yes, I do."

"Jack, m'boy, uh, would you mind?" He extended his hands tentatively toward the rock. Jack bit back an impulse to snatch it away but instead handed it to the older man and nodded as politely as he could.

A seemingly plain little rock, but this older gentleman handled it as though it was the hair trigger for a bomb. Still, Jack had seen it blast a hole in Chase's floor, so maybe it was wise for Pesky to handle it so. Pesky reverently handed it to Madame Puffin, who treated it much the same way.

Jack had been half convinced they were after him for the rock, but now it seemed they had not known of it—had no intention of running away with it at all.

"Do you know what this is, Jack?" As she said the words, Puffin stared intently at the stone, in reverie.

"A rock?" He could think of nothing better to say.

At that, Pesky let out a howl of laughter and fell to his knees, startling Jack and Chase. Puffin seemed undaunted and continued to contemplate the stone intently. She turned it over gently every now and then, moving about the room to view it under differing light.

Pesky finished howling. Jack charitably gave him a hand getting back to his feet, and Puffin handed the stone back to Jack.

Pesky wheezed, still catching his breath. "Not just any rock, m'boy."

"It is a fyrestone," Madame Puffin said, speaking the word so softly Jack was not certain he had heard her correctly.

Chapter Twenty-Two
The Rock of Ages

A what?" Jack looked at the rock in his hand.

"Perhaps not just any fyrestone," Pesky said. A wild excitement filled his bloodshot eyes.

"Pesky!" Puffin's own eyes gave stern warning.

"Well, Bea, it was the only one ever made."

"That we know of by the brothers, but in theory there could be others."

"Never. That knowledge was lost eons ago."

He turned to Jack, his face full of certainty, "M'boy, you are holding the Rock of Ages." He turned with grim satisfaction at Puffin and back to Jack with that feral light in his eyes. "The first and only fyrestone ever made. A one of a kind. The Fyrelocke itself."

"The wha?"

Puffin glared at Pesky darkly.

"I'm certain of it, Bea."

"Of that, we have no way to know, and have you considered what the timings show?"

"Yes," Pesky said. "The timing is perfect, perfect. Imagine the Fyrelocke turning up now when it is most needed."

Jack did not think Puffin's eyes could grow any darker.

"Precisely." She snorted. "Imagine that. Perhaps too perfect is the timing. Perhaps the timing is merely the priming."

Jack did not understand any of this, but it meant something to Pesky, who deflated. Fast. "Oh."

"Exactly," she said in a huff, "but I cannot think of a reason why he would send such power from on high. Such a powerful talisman in the viewing, oh. What advantage does he foresee in doing so?"

With the limited space in his room, Chase had been watching silently from his bed but finally abandoned reserve and spoke up. "Who exactly are we talking about?"

A bright flash of light, a loud poof, and Vidalia was back.

Chapter Twenty-Three
Goodbye, Cruel Room

———

I t's them," Vidalia said, breathing heavily. "The Cankrots. Watching the house with great interest." She took another breath. "There must be someone in there. The blinds keep going up and down every so often."

If it was all an act, they were very good. Jack had to admit he was beginning to believe them.

"Nah." Jack beamed. "That's just my room controller. I hooked it up to my computer, so they would think I was still in there." He turned back to Madame Puffin. "They've turned my parents into green robots, and now you're saying they sent me to get the rock? I don't think so. I think they want it."

"Relax." Puffin looked encouragingly at him, latching onto the comment about his parents. "I believe it's just a spell. One that makes your parents do their bidding well, but a spell like any other. Once the spell wears off, they should feel no bother. They will return to normal and completely. Now as to the fyrestone, discreetly—"

Pesky mumbled the word "Fyrelocke" weakly under his breath.

"As to the fyrestone," Puffin said again, "I believe it is helping you to see, as even the best of our craft cannot, something for which you are free—the spell cast on your parents to spot. Maybe the Cankrots do want (or maybe they are the ones that gave) it. It seems an odd thing to flaunt, but now you are well off to save it."

"Did you say the Fyrelocke is here?" Vidalia asked.

"Fyrestone," Puffin said, belaboring the issue. "We do not know that it is the Fyrelocke lone, but it is most certainly a fyrestone."

"No way. Can I see it?"

"Sure." Jack handed it to her. If they had been planning to take it and flash-poof out of Chase's room, they would have done it by now.

Pesky stood thoughtful for a moment. "How did you come by the Fyrelocke, anyway?"

Puffin huffed again but chose not to correct him this time.

Jack told them the story as he had told it to Chase the night before. Neither Puffin nor Pesky said much but listened intently.

At the end, Chase jumped from his bed to pull away the pile of blankets and display the gaping hole in the floor. A wave of Pesky's age-spotted hand and, with a flash of golden light, the floor magically mended.

"Thank you." Chase was beaming, more relief than awe. Jack found it odd how quickly he had given in to believing in magic. For one who had so adamantly denied the existence of it, now he accepted it without reservation. Then again, it was a bit hard to ignore at the moment—with people flash-poofing in and out of his room and flash-poofing new floors where there had once been charred wooden bits.

Vidalia turned up from the stone she was holding and asked if she could use it.

Apparent from the responses, playing with the fyrestone was a big no-no. It was immediately scooped from her palm to save her the temptation.

"No fair!"

Puffin handed it back to Jack.

He could not help wondering—if it was as powerful as they said—why they did not try to hold onto it themselves. Why return it to him, the least qualified person in the room to have a magic talisman?

"Bea, I think we should remove ourselves from this place posthaste."

"Yes, Pesky, my dear friend—and directly." She nodded. "You have never spoken more correctly."

Jack felt now was a better time for a cheery wave. "Nice meeting you."

With a wave of Pesky's hand, as if goodbye, and five accompanying flashes of light, the room emptied of its occupants. Entirely.

Chapter Twenty-Four

Wish You Were Here

———

It took a minute before Jack realized it was not so much that Pesky, Puffin and Vidalia had not left, but they had taken him and Chase with them.

He had not felt a thing. Funny, you would think a thing like being disintegrated in one place and reintegrated in another would have a little more physical sensation involved.

Making it harder to notice, they had reappeared in the exact positions from which they had left. So it was not until Jack realized there was something different about the room they were in that he realized what had happened. Seemingly, Chase had not noticed at all.

The room was surprisingly modern with blonde wood flooring, white walls and a deep yellow accent wall. The wooden furniture was darker than the floor but with smooth lines. It was definitely a living room but did not seem to fit the style of either Pesky or Puffin.

"Wait a minute. You didn't say anything about taking us with you."

"You would rather have stayed there for the Cankrots to come and collect you?"

"I haven't decided whether or not you sent them in the first place."

"Mr. Boomershine, I assure—"

"Save it!" Jack risked irreverence but did not care. If they had not been the ones to turn his parents into green robots, they had done plenty. Who were these people to chase kids down the block, pop into Chase's house uninvited and kidnap them to heaven-knows-where?

By all appearances, Pescipalius Dorfnutter was not accustomed to this kind of treatment. His deep frown made his forehead crease up and his jowls hang low, but instead of appearing dour, he looked like a gnarled tree trunk. Madame Puffin, by contrast, had a wry smile on her face.

It was right about then that Chase finally realized they were no longer in his room. He jumped up from the contemporary black coffee table upon which he had been reclining and said, "Whoa!"

Jack ignored him. "Look. I'm done with you two arguing over whether it's a lockstone or a stonelock. I don't care. I want to know who those people are that have my parents 'under their spell,' as you say, or whatever, and I want to know now."

Chase continued examining the offensive coffee table as if it had spontaneously performed the sorcery that had brought them. Vidalia looked at Jack with horror, presumably at how he was speaking to her elders, but as far as Jack was concerned, they were not his elders. They were his captors.

"Well?"

Puffin and Pesky shared a fleeting glimpse and by unspoken agreement Madame Puffin spoke. "Jack, look." She sighed and took a deep breath. "Remarkably long is the story, and we have not time in much glory."

At the cold look that came across Jack's face, Pesky interjected. "Mr. Boomershine." His voice was resonant but did not contain nearly the authority with which he had spoken earlier. "At the moment, the Cankrots are the only string we have, and should Bea and I remain here explaining things to you, we may well lose that."

Jack remained unconvinced. He wanted answers, and so far he had none.

Madame Puffin tried again. "There is so much ground to cover. Perhaps Vidalia could stay and discover to you and explain as much as she can, which should take quite a long span. Of course, Pesky and I will be back to follow up with any specifics, Jack."

Chase was nodding in the background. In the end, Jack reluctantly agreed.

As quickly as they had appeared, the two were gone.

Chapter Twenty-Five

Which Brighton?
Witch Brighton

Vidalia stood stiffly to the side, arms crossed, glaring at Jack, who suddenly had no idea what to say.

"Where are my manners?" she asked. "Oh that's right. You haven't any, so why should I use mine?" Her curly hair kept bouncing up and down. It was very distracting.

"What?"

"The way you spoke to my father. In his own house, mind you. Positively rude, that was."

"Look. Your parents barged into my friend's house and kidnapped us, and you want me to say 'please' and 'thank you'?"

"She's not me mum," she said.

"What?"

"Madame Puffin is not me mum. Me mum died some years ago. Madame Puffin is a family friend." Her tone had softened, but with cheeks reddened, her face looked as angry as it had a moment before.

"Oh, I'm sorry." Again, he did not know what to say. Instead, he pointed to the couch. "Look, do you mind if I sit down? It's been a long day."

"Certainly," she said, although she seemed only slightly happier with him sitting on the couch than she would if he were a mutant snake-man.

"Thank you."

"Oh, he does have manners."

"Really? Is that going to help anything?"

"Stop." Chase spat the word, his voice a roar. He looked back and forth between them. "Both of you. Now, look ... Vidalia? Right?"

She nodded.

"Your dad and Madame Puffin said you could help answer some questions. Maybe my friend here," he prodded Jack in the side meaningfully, "will act a little nicer if he knows what's happening." He turned his face down to the floor, licked his lips, then turned back and said, "Come to think of it, I wouldn't mind knowing, either."

All three plopped down on the couch. Vidalia let out a heavy sigh. "Well, I suppose it must be a bit disconcerting not completely knowing what is happening."

"Exactly," Chase said, smiling.

"I keep forgetting you humans aren't uncommonly clever."

"Hey! ... I think," Chase said.

"Oh. I'm sorry." She looked genuine. "I guess that did sound rude."

"Sound rude? It *was* rude," Jack said. "And you think I don't have any manners?"

"Wait a second." Chase turned to Vidalia. "Did you say humans?"

"Yes. Plainly, you are human, after all. What else could I possibly call you?"

"And you're not?" Jack asked.

"Definitely not, silly. Didn't you see all that magic? I am a witch."

"But isn't a witch a human?" Chase asked.

"Well, no, not really. Well, I suppose in the strictest sense you could say yes, but generally that term is reserved for people, um ..."

"Like us?"

"Yes. Exactly. Non-magical people."

"Ok, fine. I give up. We're human and you're not. That's totally ok by me," Jack said.

"Wow." Chase was staring and half-pointing at the window, eyes wide. "It's night."

Jack had not noticed the large window on the other side of the room. He should have—it took up most of the wall. If it had been daytime, the entire room would have been flooded with light.

"Well, not exactly. It's only about six o'clock, but it does get dark early this close to Halloween." Vidalia shrugged.

"Six o'clock? It wasn't even one when we left."

"Well, you've come to Brighton. Now haven't you?"

Aggravated, Jack asked, "So? We live in Brighton. What does that have to do with anything?"

"No. Not Brighton in the United States." She paused longer than was necessary. "Brighton, England."

Chapter Twenty-Six
Bristelmestune, the Ancient City

J ack had to sit down but realized he already was sitting down and somehow still could not shake the feeling that he needed to sit down.

Chase's mouth fell open. He looked as if, at any second, he would faint—with a bit of a greenish tinge to his face and his eyes wide. Jack had to wonder if he had that same look himself.

He took a deep breath. "Well, I guess you did say this is your house. I suppose with your accent, we should have guessed that's where we would be."

"England?" Chase asked, mumbling in Jack's direction. "She did say England, didn't she?" Without getting an answer, he turned a confused grimace back to Vidalia. "But they call it Brighton, too?"

"Well, you Yanks have a penchant for copying us and calling it your own. Being that this is a town older than America itself, I suspect we had the name first."

"I guess so," Jack said. He was finding that he did not like Vidalia very much.

Chase continued openly staring at the window. "So it takes five hours to get here? My mom must be freaking."

"It happens instantaneously. You haven't lost a second." Vidalia smiled. "There is a time difference, you know."

Somehow, in a blink, they had been popped across an ocean to a place so far away the sun had already set. Jack had trouble wrapping his brain around that. It violated several laws of physics and probably more than one international air-space agreement.

"About this being Brighton, I suppose I am not being perfectly truthful. Here, I'll show you." She shot up from the couch and walked to the veranda door, beckoning the boys outside with her.

She pointed in the distance to a small city, lights dotting the horizon. "Truly, that is Brighton." She motioned to the lights of the smaller town around the Dorfnutter household. "This is Bristelmestune, the ancient city, the foundation itself of the very city that would become Brighton."

Jack could not understand why, but it struck a chord with him. He felt a dull tingle shoot up his spine and his hair stand on end.

"What city?" Chase was looking everywhere.

"Oh, I'm sorry. You're human. It stands to reason you can't see it."

She waved her hand, showering golden sparks, and instantly his eyes lit up. "Whoa. That's too cool."

"Bristelmestune, city of magic, is hidden from the eyes of humans, who see it only as farmland." She turned to Jack. "But you saw it, didn't you?"

He nodded.

"Well, perhaps you are not fully human yourself."

He did not know why, but he took offense at that. "Or perhaps it's this dumb rock." He held up the fyrestone. "It seems to let me see things. Like the glow around my parents."

"Perhaps."

"Let's get back inside, ok? It's cold out here."

"You shouldn't be outside, anyway." She led the way back in.

Chapter Twenty-Seven
A Rhyme in Time to Divine

——

"Ok, what's with Madame Puffin?" Chase asked as the three returned to their seats.

"What do you mean?"

"Why does she talk that way?" Jack asked.

"Oh, that." Vidalia's hair bounced again. "Well, magic is all about balance, and Madame Puffin's gift is that she is a prophet. Because magic is about balance, her gift is seeing in time, and that means both forward and back. She is both prophet and historian. She has written as many historical references as she has prophetic books."

Jack looked like he was about to say something, but Vidalia cut him off. "I'm getting there. The thing is ... there are, I guess you could call them prices for her gift. One is that for anything longer than a short sentence or phrase, she is compelled to speak in lyric."

"I noticed that," Chase said. "There were a few times she didn't."

"Yes, she can use a clipped phrase or a one-word response without rhyming, but anything longer and she must. She simply cannot avoid it. We all do it. I believe even you humans do. Don't you have something called déjà vu?"

"Yes."

"What you are remembering is a time when you saw into the

64

future. You may not remember when, but you did. And the price you pay is that occasionally you will find a rhyme in your sentences over time." She crinkled her nose. "See? I'm going to have a prophetic vision soon. Anyway, humans have magic, too—not very much and not nearly as well-honed as the residents here, who have practiced for a millennium."

"You said 'one.' Are there others?"

"Well, the most obvious is the rhyme, but the second is that she is compelled to tell the truth. She can spin the truth a bit, but she cannot lie."

"Really?"

"Really."

"Ok, next question. What exactly is this thing?" Jack asked, holding up the rock. "And why do you guys all stare at it as if it's solid gold?"

"Yes, where to begin with that?" She peered around the room as if doing so would provide some clue.

"Well, I suppose the best place to start is to tell you what it is and go into the rest. Or rather, it may be easiest to show you."

Chapter Twenty-Eight
Vidalia Dorfnutter,
Geologist, Fizzicist

———

Once again Vidalia's hand flowed in an easy arc, and golden sparks flew. The lights of the room dimmed, and the rock, still in Jack's palm, took on that same strange purple glow it had when he had found it. The glow strengthened while the surface of the rock itself shimmered and disappeared.

"A fyrestone is a geode—a rock formed naturally inside the earth," Vidalia said. Aside from the surreal sensation of holding it as it lit up and shimmered, Jack had the impression he was listening to a movie at school.

Inside the rock, hundreds of purple crystal spikes pointed inward. No wonder it was so lightweight—it was hollow. The crystals kindled brightly in purple light, on fire one minute and moving as a swarm of glowing purple bees might the next.

"Geodes are basically hollow rocks, with crystalline formations inside, which form when certain unique conditions in the ground are just right. While the geode itself is somewhat rare, they are not so uncommon as to be considered a true rarity."

Chase and Jack were staring at the rock in fascination now, not unlike the way the others had earlier. *Is this what they had seen?*

"This geode is special. With amethyst crystals at its center, it is considerably rarer than most geodes. You can see how fine the crystals are."

Abruptly the lights undimmed, and the rock in Jack's hand was nothing more than a normal stone again.

"The purity of amethyst in that one is unlike any I've ever seen before," she said.

"Are you like a rock scientist or something?" Chase asked.

"A geologist," Jack said, helping him out.

"No, but ever since I first learned the stories of the Fyrelocke, I've always kind of wanted to find it. Most children do. Well, most witches anyway."

"So what's the difference between a fyrestone and a fyrerock?" Jack realized he was holding the stone more reverently than he had before. In fact, he was holding it as Pesky had earlier.

"You mean what's the difference between a fyrestone and the Fyrelocke?"

"Whatever."

"Everything," she said, taking another deep breath, "and maybe nothing. You have to understand, as far as we know, there has only ever been one fyrestone made, and that would be the Fyrelocke. If so, then they are one and the same."

"Made?" the boys asked at once, surprised.

"I thought you said they formed naturally in the earth," Chase said.

With a huff, Vidalia mumbled the word "boys" under her breath and said, "No. What I said was that geodes form naturally in the earth. Fyrestones, on the other hand, are made—albeit from geodes, but made nonetheless. Geodes themselves are common enough that you will find them polished and scattered about almost every witch and wizard household. We admire and prize them. I think even the adults secretly hope to one day find the Fyrelocke somewhere, although they would never admit to it. It's considered kind of childish to think so."

"Ok," Jack said, finding himself more than a little interested, "but why aren't they all fyrestones? Why is that one, and only that one, called a Fyrelocke?"

"Listen, do you boys want a drink? This is going to take a while, and I don't know about you, but I'm thirsty."

They answered at the same time but disagreed. Jack wanted answers, and he did not like the stalling everyone was doing. Chase was just thirsty.

"Well, I'll get three in case you change your mind."

Jack bristled. He could not help the feeling that she was patronizing them, looking down on them. Maybe he was being sensitive, considering all that had happened in the past few days. He also realized he was still worried about his parents. He could not shake the image of them in his head, imprisoned as they were.

She lifted her hand and—with another lazy wave followed by more cascading flashes—made three drinks appear on the coffee table. All three were lime green and wafted off little clouds of steam or smoke.

Chase and Vidalia immediately picked up the drinks closest to them while Jack watched. To him, the drinks looked like a potion made by some quirky mad scientist in an underground lab. He reminded himself he did not trust these people. For all he knew, the drinks could be poisoned, or maybe these were the very drinks his parents had been offered immediately before acquiring their new glimmer.

"Wow. This is really, really good." Chase had a lime green mustache. Obviously, poison had not crossed his mind. "You should try this, Jack." He garbled the words around a mouthful of the drink, trying not to let it freeze his teeth.

"These are my favorite—Frosty Forest Fizzies."

Jack shook his head. "Anyway, I was asking you why one fyrestone was a fyrestone and another could be the Fyrelocke. What makes the Fyrelocke the Fyrelocke?"

Chase was making little whimpers of satisfaction as he drank his fizzie. Vidalia was more reserved.

"Yes, yes. You're right. Well, I guess I have to explain back a bit for that."

Chapter Twenty-Nine
Of the Lockes and Their Ward

Vidalia took a deep swig of her fizzie and fell back into the couch. "Well, it all began about a thousand years ago. Back then, there was no Brighton town. Instead, there was just the small fishing village of Bristelmestune with a church on a hill and not all that much more. The town had two things that changed history. First, it was prone to invaders, being right on the coast. Second, it had the Locke family.

"By today's standards, you could hardly use the word 'rich' for them, I'm sure, but by the standards of eleventh-century Bristelmestune, they were magnificently well-off. They were well-off enough to have a keep. Not a castle exactly, although the historical references of the time refer to it as a castle, but it was probably a lot more like a small stone building than what we think of as a castle."

Jack and Chase had not said a word—both listened intently. Jack reluctantly took a sip of his fizzie, trying his best not to end up with a green mustache. Admittedly, the thing was pretty good.

"Anyway, the Locke family had two boys, Ephraim and Ignatius, and they kept a ward—an orphan boy left of the slain Cross family, who were killed in a skirmish by an invading tribe."

"The Locke brothers, and later the ward—Aaron James Cross—

would be the first to discover the powers of magic. Even by today's standards, they would ultimately become powerful, perhaps the most powerful mages there have ever been. The first and only Warlockes."

Chase cut in. "But isn't Pesky, er, your dad a warlock? A male witch?"

"No. Both men and women, boys and girls can be—and are—witches, wizards, mages and sorcerers. Those are all titles and are not gender-specific. But there have only ever been three Warlockes: Ephraim and Ignatius Locke and Aaron James Cross. There has not been a Warlocke since."

The boys took sips of their fizzies.

"Because the village was prone to invasion, the boys realized the raw power in the magic they had found and turned that power to the good of preventing warring tribes from invading their village. They called themselves the War-Lockes. Even the ward, Aaron, did.

"They experimented long and hard, trying to devise new ways to perform magic—determine its boundaries, its strengths, its weaknesses. They struck upon many of the most common spells in use today and created a classification system for those spells. They identified good magic, and discovered—and quickly abolished the use of—evil or dark magic.

"They began teaching the townspeople, who soon discovered the protection the magic offered them and overcame their fears and superstitions quickly in exchange for that protection. Not everyone could do the magic. It seemed to have something to do with bloodlines. Those who could not, moved to the outlying town—now Brighton town, which itself flourished. The tiny town of Bristelmestune was quickly forgotten—it had long since been hidden beneath the spell you now see."

Jack said, "That's all very interesting, but I don't see what any of that has to do with why Chase and I are here."

Vidalia's eyes sparkled. "Well, I don't know all of it, but I was coming to where the Rock of Ages—the Fyrelocke—comes in. At some point, the Warlockes made it but then quickly banned the making of any more. I suspect Ephraim made it. He was, after all, the dark wizard. In the oldest of texts, it is referred to as a 'stone of fyre,' or a fyrestone, or by its name 'Locke's Fyre'—the Fyrelocke.

"The details get a bit fuzzy, the history of the time not being very good, but it seems that Ephraim at some point embraced the dark magics and killed his brother Ignatius with dark magic. Aaron James Cross, the forefather of all our modern magics, avenged the wrongful death of Ignatius by taking Ephraim's life. Legend says that he used the power of the Fyrelocke to do it, whereupon the stone shattered into dust, never to be seen again.

"Some prophecies indicate that the stone was not destroyed, and that it will return in a great time of need along with the Warlocke— some descendant of the Locke family. Certain historical experts dispute that, saying that the Fyrelocke was well and truly destroyed in the skirmish with Ephraim. Further, there are no remaining members of the Locke family line anyway. The last—John, Emily and Christopher Locke—died well over a decade ago in an accident. Christopher Locke was only an infant."

"Couldn't a descendant of Cross be the Warlocke?" Jack was much more interested in the story Vidalia told than anything he had heard at school even though it sounded a lot like a history lesson. The difference was that it was a history unlike any he had heard before—and he was holding that history in his hand.

"No. As far as anyone knows, his family was killed before he became a ward of the Locke family, and he never had children. None of the Warlockes ever did. Descendants were of the Locke family but not the Warlockes themselves."

"What do the prophecies say?" Again, the fizzie in his mouth made Chase slur his words.

"Well, I know of one I can find quickly to show you."

Chapter Thirty
Don't Knock It Until ...

T hey took a quick detour through the kitchen, which did not much resemble any kitchen Jack had ever seen. There was no refrigerator, stove or sink in the room, and a large, clear cookie jar sat in the middle of the counter. It was full of spiders and centipedes, all very much alive. Although Vidalia had never left the living room to make their drinks, the sight of the cookie jar full of sprawling bugs left Jack with the offhand thought that these may be one of the feature ingredients of his Frosty Forest Fizzie.

Vidalia walked up to the counter, opened the lid, took out a small assortment of bugs and closed the jar again. Jack was half-worried she would pop them in her mouth—they were in a cookie jar, after all. Luckily she did not, but it was bad enough she was holding them. That alone gave him a shiver, and he absently scratched his arms.

As she started to leave the kitchen, Chase asked, "Um. What's with the bugs?"

"Oh these? You'll see."

The boys followed her down a redwood-paneled hall. The floor creaked beneath their steps. "Don't say a word," she said, "either of you."

As they walked, Jack could not help looking around. The little house somehow kept a balance of airiness and stuffiness. The living room was open and lively with large windows, while the hallway and back of the house were closed and dark.

They came to a set of pocket doors cracked open an inch or so. As the three came to a stop, Vidalia looked down.

"Steet your neem an' beez-ness," a small scratchy voice said with a thick Scottish brogue.

There on the floor, a few inches tall, was a gremlin. Chase quickly backed up, breathed in sharply and sounded as if he might scream. Vidalia elbowed him, and he let out a curdled yelp instead. Jack could not understand his friend's reaction. The little guy was odd-looking but not scary in the least. He had a stern round face, a slightly green tinge and wore a little suit.

"Vidalia Allium Dorfnutter and friends, here to check a book."

"Password?"

"Mausu stir fry."

"Aye, veery good. You meey enteer." The little gremlin smiled roundly.

"Hi, Knocker. I brought you some dinner." She handed him the handful of bugs she was holding.

His eyes lit up. "Aye, theenk you, Videelia. Theenk you."

"You're doing a fine job. Really."

"Theenk you," he said again and blushed proudly.

She opened the doors further and walked past the pocket-sized man, then turned to him again. "Oh, Knocker. That will be all. The master asked me to inform you that, because you are doing such a great job, you may go home for the night."

"Aye, theenk you." His face was practically bursting with pride, and he turned to leave.

After he was gone, Chase gave a little shiver and said, "Uch. That was disgusting."

Jack had to agree that the image of the little man eating spiders and centipedes was disgusting, but he chose not to say so.

Vidalia said to Chase, "You saw him as a rat. Didn't you?"

He nodded with revulsion across his face.

It had not occurred to Jack that, without the fyrestone to help him see through magic, Chase might see the little imp differently.

"Knocker is a kobold, a house gremlin. Their natural form looks much like a large mouse or a rat. You normally would never have spotted one since they pass themselves off as mice to humans." Her hand drifted over Chase, complete with the glittering light Jack was getting accustomed to seeing, and she said, "Well, you shouldn't have that problem again."

In the dim light, Jack looked around the library. Books lined every wall in heavy wooden shelves that extended to the ceiling. The stuffy air was a blend of treated leather and lemon furniture polish. A stool in the corner, a viewing table, and a worn green armchair were the only other things in the room.

"There must be some important books in here, to keep it guarded," Jack said.

"Not at all. Like mice, kobolds are house pests. The easiest way to keep them from being pests is to give them jobs. They love being praised for doing a job well, although what they really love is mice—their favorite food. As long as you keep them busy, they aren't bad. Kind of like having a smart cat. But don't ever tell them that they aren't doing their job—your life will be in mortal danger. Guarding the library is the job Knocker has been given."

She flicked her hand, and the room filled with light.

In the soft glow, Jack spotted a small strip of paper on the ground and bent to pick it up. The room remained dark enough that he did not notice the little hand that missed, by only an instant, getting to the paper before him.

Chapter Thirty-One

The Prophecy of
the Warlocke's Coming

———

Vidalia walked over to one of the bookcases, stealing Jack's attention from the paper. "Anyway, the book we are looking for is right here." She plucked it from the shelf.

With a small thud and a light cloud of dust, she placed it on the desk. "Ah, there we are."

It was a thick volume—tooled and decorated, leather-bound and aged. Jack noticed the name "Puffin" elaborately worked into the leather of the cover before Vidalia started flipping pages. "Let's see, let's see. *The Prophecy of the Blind. The Prophecy of the Aged One. The Prophecy of Perfidy and Treachery.* No, let's see. Hmmm. Oh, here, *The Prophecy of the Warlocke's Coming.*"

She turned to the page, and stood back to let the boys in. Chase read it aloud.

The Prophecy of the Warlocke's Coming

In the days before
the darkest hour,
look no more
and do not cower.
For here arrives,
anon, the one
to save thine lives:
hard fought, hard won.

The Warlocke appears,
Locke's Fyre bearing.
A state of arrears:
Bristelmestune's repairing.
The Warlocke's charge:
For ever to quell,
evil discharge,
and venom expel.

"Whoa. That sure sounds cool," Chase said, impressed, "but what's it mean?" He turned from the book to Vidalia.

"It means," Jack said as Vidalia was taking a breath to speak, "that Bristelmestune isn't the pretty little town it seems. Something evil is here—something venomous—and, after a thousand years, a Warlocke is coming to get rid of it."

Before he could say another word, Vidalia added, "And now we know the Warlocke will be here soon." She pointed to the rock in Jack's hand. "And when he comes, he's going to need that."

The voice at the door made them all jump. "Actually, Vidalia, you're wrong."

Chapter Thirty-Two
Overlooking the Obvious

Pesky stood in the doorway leaning against the frame, a smooth grin ranging over his face. At the look Vidalia gave, he softened. Even Jack realized without knowing her all that well that she would take exception to being called wrong.

"Well, I suppose 'wrong' is a harsh word, but I do think you are overlooking the obvious."

By the cast of her face, she still seemed to be overlooking it, whatever it was.

"The Warlocke, my little one," Pesky said, putting his arm on her shoulder. "It's Jack. Jack is the Warlocke."

With that, the perplexed look was wiped from her face to be replaced by one of horror. "That can't be."

"I believe he is, but enough of that for now." He closed the book of prophecy and placed it back in the empty spot between the books from which it had come. "Now, it is well past time for high tea."

He looked at the Americans in the room and amended. "Ah, perhaps I should say dinner."

They stepped out of the library and walked back down the hall to a room off the kitchen. Jack lagged behind, stunned by what he had heard. He did not know what to think and decided to ignore the comment. Pesky began to fill them in on events.

"Bea and I have been following the Cankrots from place to place as they seem to be trying to locate our Mr. Boomershine. She soon realized that it was well-nigh dinner time for me. Knowing that I can think far more clearly when not nearly so consumed by hunger, she suggested I return and get everyone fed. I, naturally, could not have agreed more."

"Nor I," Chase said, imitating Pesky's courtly tone. Despite being thin as a rail, he took his food seriously.

Pesky and Vidalia sat down at the empty dining room table, indicating chairs for Jack and Chase, who sat as directed. Jack considered mentioning there was no actual food present but settled on a wait-and-see approach instead.

"We aren't supposed to do this for meals—upsetting the balance, and all that." He looked slightly abashed. "But I think tonight qualifies as a special occasion. Wouldn't you agree, Vidalia?"

She nodded quietly, her actual agreement somewhat in doubt.

Pesky waved his arm in a circle and, with the cast of arcing golden light over the table, a full meal appeared. Roast beef on a platter surrounded by potatoes and Yorkshire puddings, gravy, bowls of cooked carrots, peas, butter and rolls, and drinks all appeared from nowhere.

Jack had no idea how hungry he was until he smelled the food, and then he was ravenous. He realized that with everything going on, he had not eaten since the day before.

The group launched into the meal with enthusiasm, and little was said. Everything was delicious. In fact, Jack had to wonder if it was the magic that made it so, or if the food overseas was that much better than what he was used to. Or if he was just hungry.

At the end, Pesky took a large gulp of wine. "Excellent!" He looked around the room at the three of them and said, "Could you go for a spot of dessert? Vidalia makes the most amazing sticky toffee pudding. You will absolutely love it."

Jack was over-full, but he had never seen Chase turn down an opportunity for dessert and his friend did not surprise him this time.

With a little huff, Vidalia cleared all the dishes—not in the conventional way—and placed in front of each of them a plate of what looked like cake with a sauce over all and a small side of ice cream. Jack wondered if the ice cream was the pudding. Then again, the Yorkshire pudding at dinner was nothing like any pudding Jack had ever seen, so maybe not.

The dessert was better than the meal: sweet, sticky and mouth-watering. Everyone seemed to love it, with the possible exception of Vidalia, who just looked bored or maybe affronted.

Chapter Thirty-Three
The Most Persuasive Argument

Finally Pesky had eaten his fill. "So what did you cover while I was gone?"

Vidalia gave a quick synopsis of their earlier discussions.

"Ah, excellent, little one. Excellent." He was the picture of contentment—with eyes half-closed, he leaned back in his chair, and his appreciable belly pushed forward.

Jack spoke up. "But I still have no idea why those people are looking for me—why they did what they did to my parents—and I don't know why you say you believe I'm the Warlocke."

"Ah." Pesky cleared his throat. "Yes. All that malarkey about the Warlocke I said before, I would appreciate it if you didn't mention it to Bea. I know she would be most upset with me if she had found I had said anything of the kind. On that, I plea the lunacy of hunger."

After a chuckle, he leaned forward, eyes keen. "As to the rest, yes, I suppose that is all true. For all that you've learned, there is so much more to know, but isn't that the stuff of life? Let us now see if we can't fill in some of those other details for you, Mr. Boomershine. Ah, perhaps the best place to begin is with the Society of All Magicks. You did not yet cover that topic, did you Vidalia?"

She shook her head sadly, her perkiness having evaporated before the meal.

"Ah, very good." His voice boomed. "Well then, let's see. The Society of All Magicks formed a few hundred years ago or so. Or I suppose it would be more proper to say that those of us uninitiated to it first became aware of them a few hundred years ago. The first documented evidence of the group comes from the early 1700s. The group is not nearly so innocuous as the name may imply. They selected the name because they embrace the dark magical arts, which are banned in all other quarters."

Chase asked the question Jack was thinking. "But what are the 'dark magical arts?'"

"Ah, true. You would not know that yet, would you? Well, Ephraim Locke—the dark Warlocke—defined dark magic before he finally turned himself to it. He defined it as 'Any magick which causes death, pain, suffering, or which uses blood or daemons as the foundation for that magick.'"

He considered for a moment and then said, "That definition is quite good, although it has broadened somewhat over the years, but the principle is basically the same. If magic causes pain or suffering—or death—as a matter of course, then it is dark magic, or black magic. It is also illegal to use any magic—dark or otherwise—for some purpose which would be considered illegal without magic, such as thievery. Merely using magic for some immoral end is, of itself, not using the dark magics, necessarily, but still immoral and perhaps illegal." He took a sip of his wine.

"The dark magic classification is reserved for those spells which have only an evil purpose and no other. Or spells which would do harm to obtain their ends. There are provisions, naturally, for using it in a time of crisis, self-defense or a time of war—which was the whole point in the first place. The Warlockes were trying to protect Bristelmestune."

"What my father is trying to get at is that the Cankrots are members of the Society of All Magicks."

"Quite right, Vidalia, the Society of All Magicks. Indeed we believe they are, and members in high-standing at that." Pesky leaned in and softened the normal rumble of his voice. "Moreover, the society as a whole—and we believe it to be relatively small—the society as a whole follows a leader. A person they refer to as the Wargothe, which I believe they intended to mean anti-Warlocke. However, its strict translation would mean they are anti-war, which is hardly the case. Nobody ever said they were particularly bright."

He cleared his throat. "Well, Mr. Boomershine, that represents roughly the sum total of what we know of the Society of All Magicks. Even that was painstakingly gathered through the efforts of the few people who have been able to temporarily infiltrate the society."

"But why only temporarily?" Jack asked. "If it was working, why not continue?"

Pesky's voice became very soft. "Sadly, death is a very persuasive argument against it. Mr. Boomershine, I may joke about them not being very bright, but they are wildly effective at that form of persuasion. Make no mistake; they are abundantly well organized and passionate in the extreme. And I assure you, the line between our people and dark magic is not the only line they will cross, and cross gladly."

Chapter Thirty-Four
False Cousins Ring True

O h, my goodness." Pesky looked at his pocket watch. "I had better get back to business and help Bea out. Before I go, boys, I do hope you will accept my invitation to make yourselves at home and spend the night tonight."

Jack and Chase both started to object, but Pesky went on, talking over them with a reassuring nod. "Until we get a better grasp of what is happening and in order to assure your safety, it would be best for you to stay here. This house will absolutely be safer for both of you than your own."

Jack was about to try again, but Pesky gave him no chance. "First, Mr. Boomershine, it is unlikely the Cankrots know you are here. But if they do, the house is warded against all uninvited magic—a Bristelmestune custom born of necessity. In a town where every citizen knows magic, a simple door lock is useless. Second, Mr. Lucre's parents have been notified that he is spending some time with his cousin. I do hope you don't mind that I've taken the liberty to arrange that."

"I don't have any cousins," Chase said.

"Hm?" Pesky said, distractedly. "Imagine that. Your parents were quite convinced you did." The way he said it left little doubt that his own directive—surely backed by magic—was behind their conviction of false cousins. Chase took on the same smile in response but only for a moment before he sobered. The seriousness of his face gave weight to Jack's own concerns.

"What about my mom and dad?"

"Jack, m'boy, I'm sure you understand they are not truly available for discussion at the moment."

They were probably still under the spell cast by the Cankrots, and trying to talk to them would be pointless, perhaps even dangerous. It might tip off the Wargothe that Jack was with the Dorfnutters. None of that changed the fact that they were his parents, and he cared about what happened to them.

Pesky finally got it from the cast of Jack's face. "Oh, yes. I see. Well, you shouldn't worry in the least about your parents. As Madame Puffin told you earlier, they will be fine. The way these spells work, your parents will be released soon—quite soon indeed. The moment they are, they should be returned to full working capacity and perfect normalcy."

Full working capacity. Great. Maybe they really are robots now.

"As I was saying, Vidalia, if you would be so kind, would you please show these boys to our spare boarding room?"

A flash of golden light filled the room as it had in Chase's bedroom earlier that day. The boys were startled, but Pesky and Vidalia turned without concern in the direction of the flash. Madame Puffin had returned.

She was harried and breathless. "Away they got from me."

"Are you ok? Were you followed?"

"No, I don't believe they found me, and I am well. Nevertheless, I suspect they knew someone was watching via spell."

"Ah, good, Bea. Well, good that you weren't followed, I mean." Pesky turned to Vidalia. "Yes, little one, now would be the time to show the boys to their room."

"Oh, of course, Daddy."

Quickly and unceremoniously, the three left the room.

Chapter Thirty-Five

A Prophecy Untold

T he room was not big, but it did have two twin beds and everything else the boys needed.

Presumably Vidalia returned to her own room, and the boys had not stopped talking since. As they were getting ready for bed and discussing the day's events, Jack remembered the little scrap of paper he had found on the ground in the library.

He pulled it out and examined it. It was old and yellowed. It had been crumpled and uncrumpled, folded and unfolded, dog eared and stained, and was cut around the edges in a haphazard shape. He turned it over and found out why. As he looked at it, it grew to the size of a normal leaf of paper, but all around the edges—tight against each outlying letter—the margins had been cut away, as if only the most important essence had been preserved and the rest discarded.

"Chase, you've got to see this."

The boys stared at the paper and the message written in flowing script.

A Prophecy Untold

A Midwife's common tale not told,
for lives, Puffin—fail not!—bold.

Swap him to the unfamiliar bed,
stop prim of each dissimilar head.
Toil vastly against lady clock.
Foil lastly—emance the baby Locke.

'Ware and mark these tiny toes,
there and hark, a Warlocke grows!

"What the heck does that mean?"

Jack shook his head as he read it again. "I have no idea."

"Same writing as in that book," Chase said, scanning it.

"Yeah, Puffin's."

"What?"

Jack looked back at his friend. "Puffin's. That book downstairs was hers—all her prophecies."

"How do you know that? Are you psychic now, too?"

Jack sighed. "No. Something far easier. I read it. On the front of the book as Vidalia opened it."

There was a loud banging somewhere in the room. Jack and Chase jumped.

Banging and thumping was suddenly all around them.

Reflexively, Jack picked up the Fyrelocke, although he had no idea how having it could possibly help him.

The noise only got louder.

Chapter Thirty-Six

Knock Some Sense into Ye

―――

The source of the banging became clear when the baseboard swung up, as on hinges, and out popped a tiny head.

Knocker, the kobold, swung his miniature frame out from the wall and scowled at them. "Theer yeh ear. Yeh scoundrels. Common theeves, yeh ear. Reff-raff an' trouble meekers."

Jack started to respond but was cut off.

"Yeh ne'er-do-weels!" The little Scottish man was obviously livid, but neither of the boys had any idea why.

There was something about a three-inch-tall gremlin, steamed and ticking, that struck Jack as funny, and he started to giggle. Chase had to laugh, too.

"Yeh see? Theer yeh be. Two o' the wors' criminals e'er to wilk the feece o' the earth. And now yeh're laughin'."

The boys could only laugh harder.

"I shoulda knewn when I firs' seen yeh. Feelthy mongrels, yeh ear."

Jack slowed his laughing enough to try and ask again. "But Knocker, what did we do that was so horrible?"

"Why, wha' didnya do? Yeh stole owny the most prized possession me very mistress gi' me."

With the kobold's accent, it was obvious Chase was having trouble following what Knocker was saying. Jack was having no trouble at all. "Mistress who? Vidalia?"

"Not mee-sis Dorfnutter. Madame Po-fin."

"Oh," Jack said. "Oh, well, what did we steal?"

"A peeper."

"A peeper?" Chase mimicked. "What's a—"

"Oh, you mean this." Jack extended the scrap of paper they had been examining. "We were, uh … We were holding it for you till you could come to collect it. I mean," Jack said, trying to think quickly. "I mean, anything could have happened to it lying there on the floor. We wanted to keep it safe for you." He handed it to the little gnome, whose face shifted from peeved to beaming in a heartbeat.

"Why, thank ye, young man." He held the worn scrap with reverence, gave it a small sniff—with which it shrank back to the size it had been—and jammed it into his little pocket. "I knew from the moment I feerst met yeh that yeh ware two o' the neecest boys I've eever met."

"Well, thank you Knocker. You are the nicest, um …" Jack had no idea if "kobold" was how Knocker identified himself. Would it be offensive? "Um, you are the nicest, too." He cringed at how flat it came out, but the little gremlin did not seem to notice.

"Yeah. I jus' knew it. I e'en said to meself … I said, Knocker— that's me, yeh know—I said, Knocker, these ear two o' the neecest boys yeh've e'er met."

It took several minutes for the kobold to repeat more or less the same thing a few times before he finally decided to leave, but he did leave in a much happier mood than when he came.

"I can't believe Madame Puffin is dating that thing," Chase said, after the kobold had gone.

"What are you talking about?"

"He said his 'mistress.'"

Jack had to laugh but immediately regretted it with the glare he got back. "He was saying mistress like his *master.*"

Chase quickly changed the subject, muttering that he was irked Jack had given away the prophecy—one they both got the distinct feeling they were never intended to see. Having read it five or six times apiece, Jack insisted that between them they could piece most of it together again from memory.

He was right. Within a few minutes, they were checking over the copy they had made. They could not be absolutely sure, but it seemed right.

Chapter Thirty-Seven

The Journey Within

The boys spent a few more minutes trying to determine what the prophecy meant but finally gave up. Within minutes, both were in their respective beds, the lights were off and Chase was already snoring.

Jack's mind flitted as he reviewed the day's events. He lay on his back and held the Fyrelocke above his face, studying it. Tonight he had seen inside it. Amazing. He had never seen anything like it. The crystals, the deep amethyst glow, how the crystals almost seemed to move as they shimmered.

Pesky's remark about him being the Warlocke popped back into his head. *It's Jack. Jack is the Warlocke. I believe he is.*

Pesky had called it the lunacy of hunger, but that explanation seemed hollow.

Could Jack be the Warlocke? If so, how? What did that mean?

Despite losing several hours in coming to England, Jack's exhaustion got the better of him. He, too, was asleep in minutes, clutching the Fyrelocke tightly in his fist.

Chapter Thirty-Eight
Locke's Fyre

W ell into the middle of the night, Jack and Chase were very much asleep. The Fyrelocke was not.

Clutched tightly in Jack's hand, it was aglow with purple light. That light grew stronger until it became so intense that the radiance itself thickened and turned into glowing purple smoke. It flowed and fused to become a murky form that stood at the foot of Jack's bed.

The boys slept on.

The translucent figure of a boy a few years older cast a purple light across Jack, who lay unaware under his covers.

He sat up straight, instantly awake, and stared directly into the phantom's eyes. The eyes stared back.

Chapter Thirty-Nine
Unlocke the Past

———

J ack scooted back in the bed as far from the ghost as he could until his back was against the wall behind him. He heard his own voice making wild grunts and yanked the blanket to his chest, as if that would provide him some meager protection.

The figure had a gentle smile on his face, and Jack knew there was no evil in that smile. In fact, if anything, it was reassuring—a knowing smile.

The ghostly figure came around the bed and held out his hand with a meaningful, imploring cast to his face. Although horror-stricken, Jack found himself driven to take the phantom's hand. There was no substance to it, but it was cool—the misty cloud formed by dry ice in water.

It must have been enough. The world spun around Jack, whirling and twisting, and suddenly stopped.

The two stood in a dusty workshop on a sunny day. High windows in the tall stone wall let in sunlight from above. Rays streamed down, chutes through the dust in the air.

Jack was having trouble focusing, like squinting through grease-smeared lenses. Although he could hear sounds, they had an odd, far-off quality, echoing and fuzzy. It took him most of a minute to

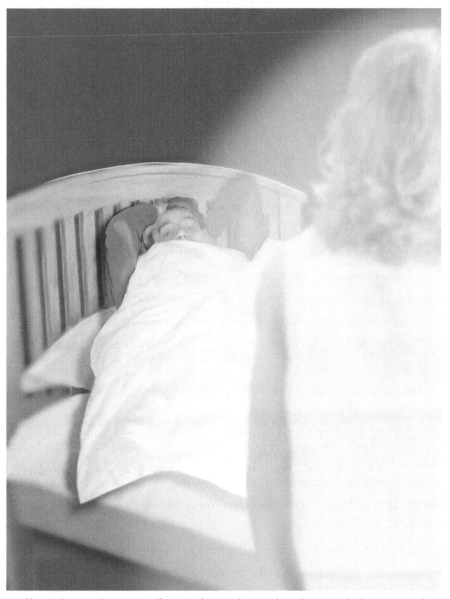

realize the noise was from three boys in the workshop moving objects across a bench, talking and laughing. "Mæg ic þē helpan?"

He could not understand a word of it.

Once his focus cleared, he realized that the tallest boy was the same as the one whose spectral hand he held, but here the boy was alive and vibrant before him. Another looked much like the first but slightly shorter, while the third was different—severe eyes and dark hair. He was the quietest and shortest of the three.

"Þū eart brægensēoc." All three were smiling and laughing, poking and punching one another good-naturedly.

The words started to become clearer. The echo of the other language they were speaking lay underneath, reminiscent of Knocker's accent, but now—somehow—he could understand the words.

"I dost not believe that will work, Ephraim," the tallest boy said with a judicious air.

The three boys were all looking at the objects on the bench, which Jack soon realized were stones—stones of all sizes, colors and shapes. He also realized that he and the boy with whom he had come were now both phantoms. He could see through his own hands.

"So pessimistic, brother Ignatius." The dark-haired one laughed, and the other boy joined him at it.

Ignatius. Ephraim. The Locke brothers—the story Vidalia had told Chase and Jack earlier that evening.

And the ward. The orphaned boy the Locke family had taken in. *What's his name again? Cross. Yes, it was Cross.*

Jack eyed the second one, remembering the story Vidalia had told them. It was hard to imagine Ephraim turning to dark magic and killing his brother. None of these boys looked like they could bring themselves to that. They were all smiling. Happy.

Ephraim shifted another stone on the bench and picked it up for the others to see. "I have high hopes for this one."

Jack immediately recognized the Fyrelocke, the rock that he held now in his own hand.

"We have tried geodes before."

"Not of amethyst, brother Ignatius." Ephraim held his head in defiance.

"Perhaps." It was obvious that Ignatius was the leader of the three.

The Cross boy spoke up. "Prithee, how dost thou know 'tis of amethyst core?"

Ephraim answered him. "I believe it is, James, because another such in the same cluster wast cracked asunder, and that wast of amethyst core." He paused, examining the small rock. "As I believe this one shalt prove to be."

Jack was trying to remember his full name. Vidalia had not called him James as Ephraim had.

It was Aaron. That was it—Aaron James Cross, she had called him.

The Cross boy took on an amused grin and said, "And with hopes our heads won't soon fill with stones, brothers."

All three of the boys laughed merrily at that. Jack did not think it was all that funny, but maybe it was funnier in the native tongue.

At that, the spinning and whirling began again.

Chapter Forty
The Making of a Fyrestone

Jack and the grim apparition of Ignatius stood in the same laboratory they had just been in, but the high windows were showing only a nighttime sky. Candles lit throughout the workshop cast only meager illumination—as many shadows as not.

James pitched a stone against the back wall, where it crashed among a pile of similar rocks. "'Tis thine turn, brother Ignatius. Perhaps thou shalt fare better."

"Aye." Ignatius jumped up to sit on the heavy stone bench. "Ephraim. Let us now try that precious gem thou hast dug and see if 'tis worth its weight in salt."

Ephraim's face lit with a broad smile. "I hope it doth not disappoint." He picked up the rock Jack knew as the Fyrelocke and placed it on a small stand not far from the head of the bench. Ignatius lay back and tried to get comfortable on the cold stone slab.

He closed his eyes, concentrating, while the other two boys stood silently by.

A moment passed. Then two. Jack felt a small flutter in the ghostly hand he was holding. Anticipation.

A bright flash of purple light erupted from the stone that was resting on the stand, followed by a purple cloud of smoke. Jack saw the screaming ghost of Ignatius ripped bodily from his form on the stone bench and sucked into the stone.

Abruptly the screaming stopped. There was silence. Purple, hazy smoke wafted up from the stone.

Jack was horrified.

Ephraim and James began cheering. Appalled at their reaction, Jack turned to Ignatius. "Why are they so happy?"

Ignatius could only stare into Jack's eyes.

"You can't talk. Can you?"

Ignatius shook his head and pointed at the stone.

Jack turned back to the scene before them, Ephraim and James dancing around the laboratory taking turns holding the stone.

Ephraim was holding it. "The power. The power is amazing. I can feel it crackle with energy." Holding the Fyrelocke in front of him, Ephraim made a rock from the bench hover in midair and, in a flash, disintegrated it—accompanied by a small burst of the purple radiance from the Fyrelocke.

Jack turned again to Ignatius as the realization struck him. "You're still in it. Aren't you?"

No response.

"They didn't see you drawn in the way I did. Did they?"

The spirit shook its head again, slowly. No.

"Brother." James got Ephraim's attention. "May I try it?"

"Absolutely." He handed the stone over.

Jack was reminded of the way Pesky, Puffin and Vidalia had all reacted to the Fyrelocke—excitement, eagerness. They all wanted to try it. Jack's own interest in the rock was much the same.

It seemed so different now. He had no idea that Ignatius' very soul was trapped inside the rock. Nobody knew. Not even Ephraim Locke and Aaron James Cross. Or at least, they did not seem to know.

After giving the stone to James, Ephraim walked over and tried to rouse Ignatius without success.

"Ignatius. Rise. Rise and see what thou hast made!" He was shouting.

James stopped paying attention to the rock and turned to Ephraim with concern. "Is he sound?"

"He breathes, yet he will not rise." A note of panic was in Ephraim's voice.

"Perhaps our brother is exhausted of all resource," James said reasonably, setting the stone down on the bench with the other fyrestone candidates. "Brother, let us move him now to his bed, that he may rest comfortably, and allow his body the respite it needs."

"Agreed."

At that, the spinning-whirling-twisting restored Jack and the spirit of Ignatius to the Dorfnutters' boarding room. Ignatius' hand released Jack's.

The ghost of the boy, whose last moments of life Jack had just born witness to, nodded once sedately at Jack and then dissolved into purple smoke. Vapors reeled, as a stream, into the rock in Jack's hand. A surge of vibration ran up his arm as the last bit of smoke was drawn into the stone.

Chapter Forty-One
Repulsion and Disgust

———

The room was dark. Only a dappling of moonlight came in through the curtains. All was still, except for the soft raspy breathing coming from the sleeping form of Chase on his bed.

Jack sat on the edge of his own, wide awake, scowling at the Fyrelocke in his hand. He filled with repulsion and disgust.

He was sick to his stomach.

Chapter Forty-Two
A Peek at the Peak of Pique

R eally?" Chase was wide awake now, too. Jack had to tell someone, and he was not about to track down anybody else in the house. "Are you sure it wasn't a dream?"

"That was no dream."

"Well, how do you know?"

"I, uh. I can't say exactly, but it was no dream."

Jack had been pacing back and forth since awakening Chase, overloaded with nervous energy. Several times now he absently held the Fyrelocke at his side until he would realize he was holding something. He would lift it to see, recognize with horror what it was, look around for somewhere to put it and realize he could not put it down. So he would hold it at his side only to start all over again some minutes later.

"I want to smash this thing against a wall," Jack said, seething.

"But what if that kills him?"

"Kills him?" He stopped pacing. "I think he's already dead. Like a thousand years ago or something."

"He wasn't dead when you saw him on the bench. He was breathing, wasn't he? Anyway, I mean, what if that destroys his soul or something?"

"I don't know." Jack was weary.

"And what about the Warlocke? I mean, isn't he kinda supposed to need it or something?"

He sat down on the bed. "I don't know. I hate this." He took a deep breath and leaned back against the headboard, motioning toward the rest of the house and the residents inside it. "I mean, I don't know if I should tell them about this. What I saw tonight didn't come close to the story Vidalia told us. Ephraim didn't kill Ignatius—no more than having a favorite rock he thought would work better."

"Work better for what?" Chase asked.

"I don't know that either. I have no idea what they were trying to do, but I don't think they were trying to do what they ended up doing."

"What?"

"Never mind." Jack took another deep breath. At least that seemed to be calming him down. "My whole point is that the story Vidalia told us tonight isn't close to what I saw with Ignatius. Which I'm pretty sure was the truth. Which means, maybe they are not our friends. Maybe they're feeding us a load so we stop asking questions."

"Maybe, but I don't think so. They don't seem like they're lying They seem like they're glad you're here."

"Not Vidalia."

"Yeah. No, not her. But Pescipalius thinks you're the Warlocke."

"He said he was mistaken," Jack said. Maybe it was from lack of sleep, or pure distaste at the image he had seen earlier, or uneasiness at the lack of control the boys had in this situation, but Jack's mood was going further down from when he had awoken Chase.

"No, what he said was not to tell Madame Puffin."

To that, Jack had no response.

It was so early in the morning that most reasonable people would yet call it night, and both boys decided to give sleep another try.

Chapter Forty-Three
A Wake-up Call

———

The first rays of the day's sunlight came in through the window and right into Jack's eyes where he lay blinking. He felt as if he had not slept at all.

Rubbing his eyes a few times, he realized that maybe he was still sleeping after all, because sitting on the bed—inches from his arm— was a creature he could not quite name. It was pure white, had immense eyes and was either large for a bunny, larger yet for a guinea pig or grotesquely large for a mouse. It looked like each of those and yet none. However, from the size of it and the long ears, Jack was thinking more bunny than anything.

Although he was startled to find this creature sitting on his bed, he was hardly shocked by it. So many odd things had been happening that, aside from pulling back a trifle, he barely reacted.

What was most peculiar was the penetrating stare with which it gazed at him. That—and the fact that it was sitting as a person would, rather than lying on its belly as a rabbit might—left little doubt that this was no house pet.

"Well, good morning." Jack thought it worth trying. The creature did not respond in any way except to slowly blink its large crystal-blue eyes and raise its ears halfway.

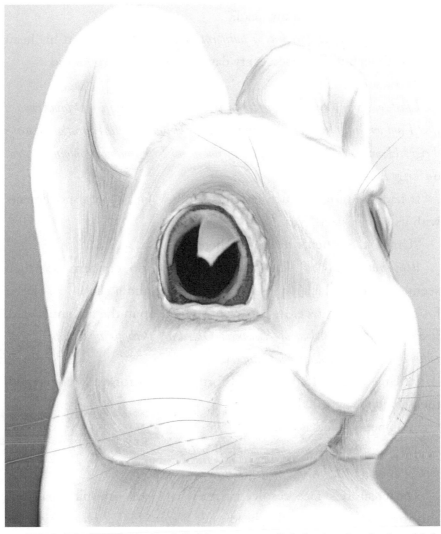

"Um. My name is Jack." He sat up slightly in the bed, which jounced. The creature stared wide-eyed at him in return.

Abruptly, the words "Pleased to meet you" floated as a squeaky British voice through Jack's head.

My name is Trygg.

For a second, he thought he was hearing things, but the creature's mouth had not moved other than to accommodate a slight twitch of its nose.

"Uh. Did you talk in my head?"

Naturally. It's the only way a puriform can talk, the voice in his head said, as though it happened every day. Perhaps for Trygg it did.

"Who are you?"

I just told you. Trygg the puriform. As if being a puriform is not proof enough that I am one, indeed. And my name is Trygg, of course. Did I mention that it's Trygg? However, truly it is Tryggth, but you might have trouble pronouncing that. So Trygg is fine.

It had not moved much except to follow Jack's own movements with its saucer-sized eyes.

"Um. Ok. So then why are you here?"

Why wouldn't I be? The creature showed no concern but then seemed to weigh Jack's question a little more and a slightly panicked look came over its face. Its ears went straight up in the air, and it said, *Wait. Was I supposed to be elsewhere? Oh, dear! Perhaps in Caulpers? No, today is Sunday. Certainly not Caulpers.*

Its large eyes shifted back and forth, looking forlornly concerned, then genuinely worried.

"Caulpers?" Jack asked.

Yes. Caulpers. Almost the same as Whatsis—only different. Oh my. Did I miss Whatsis? I hate when I miss Whatsis.

The creature's face resolved somewhat, ears drooping halfway, and the little voice in Jack's head said, *Well, if I've missed it, there is no point in going now.*

The creature turned to look Jack in the eyes.

"It's pretty early to be anywhere, isn't it?" Jack tried to reassure the little puriform.

Ah, but time—and place, for that matter—are relative to where you are. Aren't they? It was more of a statement then a question. *Bright early morning here is the dead of night where your parents are.*

At the mention of his parents, Jack bristled.

Trygg looked thoughtful, ears flattened against its head. *They are ok. No worries. Perhaps we should hurry, though.* The little creature extended an arm toward Jack, presumably to help him up—not exactly a paw, nor was it a hand, but somewhere in between.

Jack took it, and the two transported to a stuffy little room, visible only because of the dim red glow of an exit sign.

Chapter Forty-Four
A Puriform Suite

———

The air was stale, steeped with the twined scents of dust and must.

"Where are we?" Jack said in a hushed voice—the room seemed to dictate that he should whisper.

With no apparent prodding, the lights came on, though dimly. Trygg motioned at a sign on the wall as a game show host might have.

Brighton City Hospital
Department of Records

Beneath the plaque was a small sign that read, "Under no circumstances shall any original document leave this office."

No sooner had Jack read the signs than Trygg started scampering about the room, squeaking frenetically. The little creature bounded between file cabinets and bins, storage units and shelving. It capered up the side of one, along the length of another, and back down along the ground, squeaking and screeching in stride.

Jack was certain the noise would bring someone to investigate, but no one came. He could only watch with no idea what was going on or why Trygg had brought him here.

The creature continued for some time before the little puriform came to rest two floor tiles in front of Jack. It calmed and held its arms up and out, as an orchestral conductor might. While its bunny-nose was cast toward the ground, its ears were straight up and rigid. Slowly, the little white puriform moved its arms and ears around in an odd pattern—also reminiscent of a conductor in a symphony hall. At each motion, instead of music, file cabinets throughout the room opened and closed, cabinet doors swung open, and storage lids popped off and resealed. The sound was musical, with a pattern and precision all its own. Each click was in rhythmic succession or in accompaniment to a screech, a squeal or a shuffle of papers: Trygg was conducting a puriform suite.

Slowly, sheaves of aged papers came floating from throughout the room. As they floated by, they came to rest on the corner of an information desk near Jack. The pile quickly got taller.

The boy stood mesmerized by the dance of papers, pages and folders as they meandered through the air and came to rest on the pile at unspoken direction from the little white puriform, just a few feet tall, standing in front of him. Each movement—of arms and ears—was punctuated with a little squeak from Trygg.

By the time the whole thing was finished, the pile was sizable—several reams thick. Jack peered over the stack and caught a glimpse of birth records and death certificates. A sharp snap echoed throughout the room. The large bundle of papers was bound like a stack of newspapers.

Trygg finished with a flourish and beamed happily.

Jack stood speechless.

Well?

"Well, what?"

Well, what did you think?

"Um. It was pretty cool."

That's it? Pretty cool? I saved you from hours of toil and drudgery, and I did it as a master of the arts, and all I get is "cool"?

"Um, thanks?"

Trygg sniffed grumpily. *Well, take them and let's be off, then.*

"Take them? I don't think I could lift them." He eyed the bundle with doubt.

Trust me, would you?

Jack was about to argue but decided to give it a try.

The bundle lifted as easily as a small manila folder.

See? You can put your trust in Trygg. Ok, now let us depart.

"Wait." Jack was mortified once he realized the puriform intended to take the papers with them. He pointed at the little sign on the wall.

Oh, don't worry. That's not for us. That's for the riff-raff.

Without warning and any hint of movement, Jack was standing in the bedroom alone—except for Chase, who slept placidly in the early morning light.

Chapter Forty-Five
A Bundle of Surprises

I'm still not getting this." Chase rubbed the sleep from his eyes. "Some little white furball woke you up and took you to the hospital, so you could steal a giant pile of papers. Right? But why?"

"I didn't steal anything."

"I thought you said you took them."

Jack growled. "I was carrying them, but I had no idea Trygg would pop us out of there so fast."

Chase's hair was frizzed from sleep, his pajamas a disheveled mess—but so was his bed. He sat amid his rumpled blankets staring into his hands. "So why did you steal the papers again?"

"I didn't steal anything. The puriform gave me these to take back here, saying it had 'saved me from hours of toil and drudgery.'"

"I thought you said the bunny never talked."

Jack was getting irritable. "It wasn't a bunny. It was a puriform. And right, it never talked exactly, but I could kind of hear its voice in my head."

Chase whistled. "Jack, old pal, you should have stayed in the hospital."

"Chase, c'mon. This whole thing …" He growled again instead of finishing.

Chase sat back on the bed and tilted his head toward the ceiling. "So let me get this straight. Not once, but twice last night you got visited, and both times I happened to be sleeping. Once was by a ghost and once by a furry bunny rabbit that could talk in your head—though it never made a sound."

Jack had to admit it sounded funny, but humorous or not, Chase was getting him riled. "Three things. First, we were not visited twice last night. We were visited three times—you're forgetting about Knocker, who you were not conveniently asleep for. Second, Trygg did make sounds, just no words. Other than that, you've pretty much got it. And third, it's not my fault you could sleep through the Tunguska meteor."

"The what?"

"Never mind."

"So what is all that stuff anyway?" Chase pulled himself from the bed to get a closer look.

"A bunch of hospital records." Jack was fumbling with the bundling straps but could not get them to budge.

"And you needed these because … ?"

"I have no idea. You know as much as I do now."

Finally Jack found it—a little release on one of the straps. He disengaged it, and it was as if all the magic holding the bundle together suddenly let loose. Papers cascaded to the floor in all directions, some springing all the way across the room.

"Nice."

"I had no idea it'd do that."

"I noticed."

"Ok, help me pick this stuff up. Would you?"

The two boys bent down to reorganize the papers, but it was questionable how well organized the bundle had been in the first place.

"Hey," Chase said.

"What?" Jack's voice was muffled. He was trying to reach some papers that had fallen under the bed.

"It's your name, Boomershine." Chase was holding up a small card. "Zatch-a ... Zatch-air-ee-ah. What is that?"

"What? Let me see that."

Sure enough, the card contained Jack's name among other things.

Baby Boy Boomershine

Born:	13 December, 6:37AM
Weight:	7 lbs., 8 oz.
Length:	19 in.
Mother:	Carly Anne Boomershine (nee Smith)
Father:	Walter C. Boomershine
Midwife:	Mme. T.B. Puffin

At the bottom of the card was handwritten "Jackson Zachariah Boomershine."

"That's Zachariah," Jack said distastefully. This was not the kind of thing you wanted your friends to see. "Zack-a-rye-ah."

"Really? Oh, that's great." Chase's smirk was pure evil. "And Jackson?"

"Yeah." Jack just shook his head.

"Wait. That means you're Jack-Zack?" Already trying to come up with ways to get under Jack's skin, Chase said, "This is great."

Chapter Forty-Six
It's All in the Cards

J ack inspected the card. It had a slight, though distinct, green glow around the edges and smeared across the front. He knew Chase was unable to see that. "Wait. I was born here?" He made a mental note to ask his parents about that when they were normal again. They had never mentioned he was born in England. "What's a midwife?"

Chase made the universal I-don't-know sound and shrugged. He was already back to picking up papers.

"Madame Puffin is listed as the 'midwife.'"

"What?" Chase came back to look again. "Holy cow, you're right. Does that mean she's related to you?"

Jack found the entry in his smartphone dictionary. "One who aids in delivering a baby," he read it aloud. "Wait a minute." Jack pulled the paper from his pocket containing the *Prophecy Untold.*

"Yes," he said, pointing at the prophecy. "It says, 'A Midwife's common tale not told.'"

"What?"

"I don't know. There's something about that. Puffin writes a 'Prophecy Untold' that features a midwife swapping a baby to the 'unfamiliar bed.' Then she is the midwife at my birth. There's

116

something there," Jack said excitedly, flipping through the rest of the papers on the desk and on the ground.

"Great. It all seems so clear now." Chase grimaced but quickly added, with a wicked grin, "Jack-Zack."

Jack ignored him and continued riffling through a stack on the desk. "I think, um. I wonder if that prophecy was an instruction note to Puffin, telling her to switch two babies. And one of the babies is the Warlocke."

Chase began rereading the prophecy with interest.

"Wait, this might be it." Jack had found another card similar to the birth notice they had found with his own name on it. "Yes. Yes, it is!"

Baby Boy Locke

Born:	13 December, 8:42AM
Weight:	7 lbs., 8 oz.
Length:	19 in.
Mother:	Emily Sooth Locke (nee Sanders)
Father:	Jonathon Reginald Locke
Midwife:	Mme. T.B. Puffin

As before with his own card, the baby's name was written by hand across the bottom—"Christopher James Locke."

This card had the same fading traces of a green tinge. That made Jack nervous. The only other time he had seen the green glow was as a halo around his parents, and he knew they were being forced to lie—to pretend to go along with whatever they were directed to do.

Could the cards be trusted? If so, they held the answer.

He quickly scanned the papers spread across the room but did not spot the green glow anywhere else.

"I don't get it." Chase stood with his mouth open, staring at the card Jack had found.

"Well, if it's true, it means that Christopher Locke didn't die in a car crash so many years ago. It means that 'Baby Boy Boomershine' did." Jack looked wild-eyed but went on. "The real Jack Boomershine."

"What?" Chase now took on that same wildness in his eyes. "How do you get that from this?"

"Chase, it's all there. They both have the same midwife, the same weight, the same length, and they were born two hours apart. On top of it all, the prophecy says, 'Swap him to the unfamiliar bed.'" He brushed his hand through his hair. "I think she did it. I think she did it, and now—somehow—someone knows."

"Did what? And who knows?"

"Me. I think she swapped me for the real Jack Boomershine. Chase, I think she wanted to protect Christopher Locke, and she did it by swapping the two babies. I think I'm Christopher Locke."

Jack was looking at the green smudges on the card. "And I think now, somehow, the Wargothe knows."

Chapter Forty-Seven
A Radiant Hypothesis

——

The minute he said it, he knew it was true. It left a crushing feeling in his chest. It meant his whole life had been a lie. His parents were not truly his parents. The life he had known was never really his. It also meant so much more than that. For better or worse, he was the Warlocke—he had magic in him. He would have to find it.

He also knew that the Wargothe knew. The fading green glow on the cards made sense now. The Wargothe had found out somehow—had found the same cards that Chase was now poring over.

"Whoa, so you are the Warlocke?"

"I think that's what all this means." Jack swept his hand over the two birth cards and the prophecy.

"Ok. So then why did the furball stick you with all this other stuff?"

Distractedly, Jack ignored the question. "You know, I think there's one way to find out for sure. I mean about being a Warlocke."

"What?"

"Well, a Warlocke has to be magical and has to be pretty good at it, right?" Jack stacked the cards and the prophecy and put them with the other papers.

"I guess. Sure."

"Well, I'll get Vidalia to show me a few things, and we see how I do. If I'm a Warlocke, I should pick right up. In fact, I should probably be better at it than she is. Right?"

"Um. Yeah. Probably." Chase did not look so sure.

"Here, help me finish picking this stuff up."

They organized the heap of papers so they were stacked, more or less, as they had been before Jack snapped the bundling cord. After hiding the mass of paperwork in the closet, the boys left the room.

Chapter Forty-Eight
Rumbled, Tumbled

W ell, I want to try it and see if I can do it."

Vidalia looked less certain than Chase had.

Jack considered telling her everything—the three visitations, the prophecy, the birth records—but he could not bring himself to do it. He did not know why, but he thought it best to keep it to himself for a while. Besides, what if he ended up not being able to ... to ... what if he just could not do it? Vidalia would make fun of him for thinking he was the Warlocke in the first place.

"But you're a human," she said.

"I know, but you said yourself I might have some magic."

"Well." Her hair bobbed up and down as she shook her head, but she had a wry smile on her face. "Oh whatever. It couldn't hurt to try. You sure you want to?"

"Yeah."

"Do you want to try, too?" She pointed at Chase, whose lanky form sat reclining in a chair, watching them both. They were back in the living room, in roughly the same places they had been in the night before.

"I'll see how this turns out first." He smiled.

"Suit yourself." Vidalia turned back to Jack. "Ok, let's start with something—"

"Flying … I want to try flying." He had calculated that. He wanted to either prove or disprove being a Warlocke, and he was not going to do that with some easy start-up task, which he knew she would pick first. He had decided to circumvent that whole thing by forcing the issue.

"Flying? No way. Even if you have magic, that's far more advanced than you should attempt on your first go."

"Well, hovering. Not flying exactly. I mean, we're in your living room, right? How far could I fly?"

"No, I don't think that's a good idea. I mean, witches and wizards that have been doing magic for years—"

"Oh come on, Vidalia. You said yourself—what could it hurt? Let me try it."

Her face turned red. "Fine. Fine!" Obviously not fine. "But if you break your neck, don't say I didn't warn you."

Chase piped up. "If he breaks his neck, I doubt he'd say much of anything."

Vidalia glared at him.

"Ok, let's get this over with. For the record, I say there is no way you're the Warlocke. So I hope that's not what you have in mind. With that said, the first thing you have to do is think about what you want to do. So picture yourself hovering in the room here."

"Ok." Jack closed his eyes.

"You don't have to close your eyes."

"Oh. Ok. But how do I picture anything with my eyes open?"

"Fine. Close your eyes."

He closed his eyes again. "Ok, now what?"

"Well, that's it."

"What's it?" Jack opened his eyes again and gave her a hapless look.

"Picture what you want to do."

"But what's the next thing?"

"There is no next thing. That's it," Vidalia said.

"You said 'the first thing you have to do,' which means there's a next thing. There's no next thing?"

"No."

"Really?" Jack stared at her, his hand out.

"Really."

"So my whole life I could have had magic and never even known it?"

"Really."

"There has to be more to it than that. Isn't there?"

Vidalia stood motionless. "Well, sort of. Two things, I guess. First, you have to picture whatever it is you want to do. I mean picture it. In full detail. Crisply. Clearly. Second, you also have to believe it. You have to know that you can do it and not question yourself. That's the hard part. If you think you can't do it, then you won't, but there isn't much more to it. I mean, after you master that, then there are little shortcuts I can teach you. Like how to use less energy to do different things. That's pretty much all there is."

"Wow." He had no idea what to say to that. He had expected a lot more to it—spells he would have to learn, incantations to master. He never expected it would be so easy. "Ok. Um. I guess I'll try again, then."

"Ok," she said with a smirk.

After licking his lips, he closed his eyes once again, stood with his hands out from his sides and … Nothing happened.

He stood that way for a full minute, and still nothing.

"Flying is tough," Vidalia cut in. "Maybe focus less on flying and picture that you are as light as the air itself. You have to give in to it. Feel yourself becoming as light as the air. Feel it beneath you, carrying you up."

Chase rolled his eyes.

Jack tried again.

After a minute, this time something happened.

Waving his arms wildly to stop from falling over, Jack leaned back to catch himself and tripped on the coffee table. Chase and Vidalia both laughed as Jack lay seething in a heap on the floor.

"Sure you don't want to start with something a little easier?" Vidalia asked.

"Well," he said, getting up and brushing the hair back from his face, "I guess we could try something that's maybe not quite so advanced."

"Yes." She helped him stand up. "Good idea."

Chase cut in. "I wish I'd thought of it."

Chapter Forty-Nine
Humbled

———

Vidalia ignored Chase's comment. "Probably the easiest thing to do is a deflection."

"A deflection?"

"Yes. Um. It's where you push away a spell someone directs at you." She mimed throwing a ball at Jack and batting it down. "You don't need much magic to be able to deflect a basic spell. There are ways I can stop you from deflecting them, though. And some of the more advanced spells are surprisingly hard to deflect, but I won't do any of that for this, uh, attempt."

"Ok. So what do I do?"

"Pretty much the same thing—picture the spell bouncing off of you."

Jack closed his eyes again.

After a small flash of light, he felt a little fuzzy-headed and heard Chase guffaw. Vidalia joined in laughing a second later.

"Qwhat!" His voice was muffled and rough. He opened his eyes, and the world around him was huge. So was his nose. It was enormous, and it had a sheen to it.

He looked up at the two gigantic forms of Vidalia and Chase chortling in a room similar to the room they had been in moments before but far more massive, unable to comprehend what was going on.

"You're a ... you're a ... *a chicken!*" Chase could barely get the words out through his laughter.

"Qwhat?" Jack asked to no effect from Chase and Vidalia.

"Ah, hang on," Vidalia said through tears of laughter. She waved her hand, golden sparks fluttered down on him, and everything was back to normal. Normal except for a few stray feathers wafting to the ground and the fact that the two were still laughing raucously.

Once they had calmed themselves, Vidalia—completely unnecessarily by Jack's estimation—explained that his deflection could probably use a bit of work, at which the two erupted into laughter again.

After that, things went downhill.

Vidalia consecutively turned Jack into a frog, a groundhog, a dog and—most unfortunately—a hog. That last left neither Jack nor the living room in a very good condition upon his return to Jack-ness.

Both needed some airing out afterward.

Chapter Fifty
Late Bloomer Shines

———

Jack sat humiliated in the room he and Chase had been given, as dour as someone could be who had experienced much of a zoological nightmare in such short order.

He had felt nothing. No hint of magic at all. No tingle, no light-headed sensation. Nothing.

After a few minutes, Chase joined him. "You ok?"

"Yeah," Jack said, but he knew it was obvious he did not mean it.

"You know, it doesn't mean anything."

Jack looked him in the eyes. "Actually, I think it does. I'm no Warlocke, Chase. I've been thinking about it, and I'm the exact opposite of magic. I know mechanics, electronics, computers and chips. I know servos and motors, and doo-dads—as Mom and Dad like to say. I know capacitors, resistors and diodes, and three different computer programming languages—all the things of which witches and wizards have no need. I think it does mean something. To be honest, I'm glad for it. Now I get to keep my parents, and all their greenness. I get to keep the life I know. I may not be a Warlocke, but I'm a Boomershine, and that's all that matters."

"Exactly." Chase looked at him and smiled. "Smart, very smart."

Jack stood up to go, but Chase stopped him. "You know what I think is the funniest thing?"

"What?" Jack said, mildly annoyed, not wanting to hear about which particular animal was the funniest.

"I think it's funny that you—the guy who is so good at magic tricks—has absolutely no potential with real magic."

A big smile floated across Jack's face. He had not expected that, certain Chase would hit him with something funny that had happened while turned into a gerbil. Not that he *had* been turned into a gerbil, as far as he knew.

"Yeah, maybe I should show Vidalia some sleight of hand. Now there's magic."

Chase loved Jack's sleight of hand, giving the impression an object had disappeared, though he had palmed it. He asked Jack to do it constantly. Everyone in school was fooled by it.

Jack started from the room.

"Where are you going?"

He poked his head back in the door. "I know what I know, but I still want to talk to Puffin."

Chapter Fifty-One
A Hero for the Masses

A m I, or am I not, the Warlocke?" Jack stood defiantly before Madame Puffin, chin out, eyes fixed on hers. He wanted an answer.

He had found her in the study. No kobolds were on guard duty at the moment.

"You have not quite surmised correctly, but by prophecy rite I cannot answer so directly," Madame Puffin said in her familiar singsong tone.

"But—"

"Nevertheless, there are things I can say, and as to those, I will tell you this very day." Gently, she brushed a bit of hair from his forehead and gave him a wink and a nod.

She took a heavy breath and let out a sigh. "You think a Warlocke you may be, but I tell you that soon you'll see. A real Warlocke out there passes"—she gave a small wave at the room's window—"the hero, somewhere, for the masses. The Warlocke you'll see with your very eyes, and only then will you realize: In all of this, your own role—the path you ride with your very soul. Now Jack, good child, we will talk again soon. Please, though, get some dinner. 'Tis well past noon."

He had only half-heard what she said. Madame Puffin had a way of making him feel like he was being read a nursery rhyme—like a chant, it mesmerized him. Aside from that, his brain shut off the minute he realized she was saying he could not be the Warlocke, since—silly boy!—the Warlocke is still out there.

He decided to head back to the room and get Chase. Although he was not particularly hungry, he knew he should be. Maybe it would help clear his mind.

He knew he should be happy to find that his parents were still his parents, his family still his family and his life still his life. But for some reason, a part of him was disappointed. Although he did not want to lose any of those things, he did want to find out that he was special in some way.

The morning had felt like a roller-coaster. Up, down, up, down. Now, again, he felt down. Definitely down.

On top of it all, his parents were possessed. He worried constantly for their safety and had no real understanding of what was happening around him.

His footfalls were harsh against the wooden floor on his way back to the room.

Chapter Fifty-Two
Doddering about with a Wimple

——

The three—Jack, Vidalia and Chase—were eating lunch in the dining room, some simple sandwiches, when the doorbell rang. Vidalia was about to get up when Pesky walked by in a daze and nudged her shoulders down, signaling for her to remain seated.

As they sat and ate, they could hear the door open and Pesky's rich voice. "Ah, Mr. Wimple, Mr. Dodder. So good to see you again."

"Pescipalius, good friend," an older man said.

"And is that Madame Puffin?" another man asked, his voice an rough but slightly different in tone. "Ah, Bea, I have not seen you for ages."

"Not since the last meetings three, to be sure, that I say with complete certainty," Madame Puffin said.

Laughter issued all around, but it was stiff. There was a purpose to the visit, and it was not for small talk.

Pescipalius spoke next. "Ah, whom have we here?"

Wimple, or maybe it was Dodder, answered. "Well now, Pescipalius, that is the matter …"

"… For which we have come," the other finished.

"I do wish you would stop interrupting me," the first voice said. "You do that incessantly, and it is most infuriating."

"Only because I am right. You hate being wrong. Besides, you interrupt me as often as I do you."

Madame Puffin's voice cut in. "Ah, young man, perhaps to the kitchen with me you will come. I've just now made dinner, and I do hope you will have some." There were shuffling noises as the two left the room for them to hash out whatever it was they had to hash out.

Vidalia put a finger to her lips and looked squarely at Jack and Chase in turn. It was unnecessary, as neither had any intention of making a sound.

Pesky resumed. "Now what's this, Wimple?"

"Well, Pescipalius, it is difficult to explain," the older man said in a hushed voice but clear enough to be heard in the dining room.

Dodder said, "Some days ago the boy was found wandering a rural road. He has not spoken a word. Not then or in the time since."

"He was taken to the hospital, where he checked out fine," Wimple said.

"To be sure, that is only physically," Dodder added.

"However, I'm not in the least bit certain of his mental state." Wimple finished.

Pescipalius halted the back-and-forth. "Why, then, have you brought him to me?"

There was silence for a moment. Finally a Dodder or a Wimple spoke up. "Well, what else can we do? You are, by far, the most powerful among us, and ..."

"... And we had jolly hoped you could get through to him."

"Find out who he is."

"What has happened to him."

"Where he belongs."

It was amazing. The two older men bandied back and forth as if they were of the same mind. Jack conjured an image of a two-headed man holding the conversation with Pesky in the other room.

"What?" Pesky said, not happy in the least. "I have my hands beyond full at the moment, my dear friends. You are well aware of the situation at present, as I know I have apprised the council most thoroughly."

"Well and true, old friend, but …"

Wimple let out a shrill cry. "Ouch! That was my foot! Why don't you watch where you step, you doddering old dolt?"

Dodder, offended, lit in. "Well, at least I'm not named for some ridiculous woman's headdress. Besides, if your feet weren't each as large as wolverines, perhaps they could be avoided without much measure of difficulty."

"Gentlemen, gentlemen," Pesky said. "Please, may we continue with the matter at hand?"

Dodder began again, "As I was saying before being irascibly provoked …"

Wimple murmured something under his breath about his maimed foot.

Dodder went on. "… Well and true, Pescipalius. We know you have your dance card full at the moment, but …"

Wimple finished for him. "… Perhaps this, then, is exactly where this young man is supposed to be."

"What?" Pesky sounded even less happy with that suggestion. "Surely you must be joking."

Wimple or Dodder spoke up. "Joking is …"

"… and never has been …"

"… one of our strong suits …"

"… as you well know, Pescipalius."

The veiled threat surprised Jack. He had assumed Pesky was pretty high-ranking in the council, but it seemed there were others higher.

"Yes, yes. Yes, I understand." Pesky's voice dropped a note. "The boy can stay briefly. But to this I object, and I plan to make that objection clear at the next council meeting. Surely you must see the importance of allowing me to focus my attentions just now."

Chapter Fifty-Three

A Stranger, Stranger Still

After some less contentious small talk, the older men left. Vidalia, Chase and Jack heard nothing more and went back to finishing their lunches. Jack was not very hungry and had only picked at his.

"Wow. Those two old guys hate each other," Chase said after taking a drink of his Frosty Forest Fizzie.

"Mr. Dodder and Mr. Wimple?" Vidalia laughed. "Not really. I know what you mean, though. I used to think so, too, but they're inseparable. I used to wonder why they didn't stop being friends, but then I realized that they don't hate each other at all. That's how they are. They've been friends longer than Daddy has been alive."

There was little conversation after that. Jack lost himself in considering what Madame Puffin had told him—that the real Warlocke was out there somewhere. She had made it very clear that he would see the Warlocke and then he would know what his own role would be.

That was fine, but right now he had no idea—not who the Warlocke was, and not what his own role would be. That, and his concerns about how his parents were faring under the spell in which they were trapped, weighed heavily on him. He poked at his sandwich but did little more than that.

Before long, Pesky and Puffin entered the room with a very thin boy in tow.

He was about the same age as the others, with striking, dark, straight hair. His pale white skin had a milky, translucent quality to it that made him look sickly. He never looked up but kept his eyes focused sadly on the floor.

"Hello, everyone," Pesky said. "We have a new guest staying with us for a while. I'm afraid I do not yet know his name, but I am hoping that in due time he will judge us well enough to trust with it. In the meantime," he turned to look at the boy, "I believe I will call you *young man* if that is amenable to you."

The young man gave no indication of having heard. Madame Puffin introduced the others to him, but again he did not respond with even a nod.

He was quickly ushered off to a guest room of his own, leaving Jack to wonder how many spare rooms the house held.

After the boy and Puffin left, Pesky stayed behind to talk to them. With the boy safely gone, Chase said, "That kid could use a meal or two."

Vidalia stuck up for the nameless young man. "Perhaps he could have a number of yours. You surely could do without."

Chase was almost as thin as the newcomer, but you would never know it to watch him eat. He could put food away at an alarming rate.

Pesky interrupted. "Listen, I want you to know something, but I am going to ask you not to repeat this to him and frankly use discretion when discussing with anyone. That young man has experienced something very traumatic—cognijectus severus—a dark spell that completely erases all or almost all memory."

In astonishment, all three spoke at once, but Pesky cut them off.

"Yes. It was done to him on purpose. A spell like that could hardly happen by accident, Vidalia," he said with bitter distaste. "I don't know who would ever do such a thing. I can hardly imagine, Jack." He answered each of the three in turn. "And no, Chase, I did not sneeze, but thank you just the same."

He cleared his throat. "You should know that he cannot remember much, and at the moment I wonder if he can recall how to speak. It is entirely possible that he does not remember even that or perhaps his own name. Anyway, you will have to go easy on him. Don't ask too much of him. At best, that spell is extremely traumatic. At its worst, speaking is the least of one's problems." He mulled that for a moment before continuing. "At its worst, the victim may forget how to eat, drink or even breathe. It is a horrible spell. I cannot fathom using it on anyone, let alone a mere boy."

Pesky finished what he was saying and then left the room amid a grim cloud, his responsibilities having quickly doubled.

With little else to do, the three cleaned up the mess they had made. None of them had eaten much, except for Chase, of course.

Chapter Fifty-Four
A Room Devoided

———

Being a girl, Vidalia got it in her head that visiting the new boy in his quarters would be a nice thing to do. Jack was not sure what would be nice about it. The kid hardly seemed nice enough to want to visit in the first place, and a charitable visit seemed as if it would scarcely be well received.

Wary, Jack and Chase went along anyway.

"Hello," Vidalia said politely as the boy opened the door to their knock, eyes still on the floor.

"My name is Vidalia."

"And I'm Jack."

There was silence until Jack kicked his friend's shoe. "Er, and I'm Chase. Nice to meet you."

Silence.

"Mind if we come in?" Vidalia asked, moving her way past the boy.

As they walked in, they could see that the room had been changed. Even Jack, who did not know how it had looked before the young man had been given the room, got some sense of the transformation.

The curtains were almost closed with only a small hole toward the top. The bed had been moved against the wall so it would be across from the door and adjacent to the window—surely not where it had been. It had also been stripped down to the bare mattress. The bed linens and everything loose in the room appeared to have been put in the closet, which was now so jammed with knick-knacks that the folding doors bulged.

The room looked spartan now—devoid of anything that may have once given it some feeling of life.

It seemed a prison.

Vidalia stuttered a few times as she asked, "Are you finding you like it here?" She did not mention the state of the room.

Jack and Chase did not know what to say, so they stood by, fidgeting.

Vidalia changed tacks. "Um. Well, we wanted to let you know that you're welcome here, and if there is anything you need, please ask. If you're not comfortable talking, try and give us some idea of what you may need in any way you can, and we will do our best to help. Ok?"

Still no answer.

Jack spoke up. "Ok. We'll let you relax now. Yell if you need something." He started pushing Chase back toward the door.

They let Vidalia out first. Chase followed. As Jack was about to walk out the door, he turned to look at the boy, who was staring directly into his eyes.

With the vibrant green in those eyes—the only splash of color anywhere for the kid—Jack was struck with a thought. *The Warlocke.*

Jack waved and left the room, closing the door behind him.

The three walked a few paces down the hall as Chase muttered under his breath. "Whoa, that kid is weird."

Jack was thinking about the sensation he had while in the room. *No way. No way. There is no way that kid could be the Warlocke.*

139

Yet for some reason, in an absurd way, it kind of made sense, but it was ridiculous. Of all the people who could be the Warlocke, this "young man" was probably the only one less qualified than Jack himself—at least by appearances. But appearances could always be deceiving.

Jack filed the thought off into the back of his head. He would have to think that through later.

Chapter Fifty-Five
Better than a Nose-ectomy

H e did not know about Vidalia or Chase, but the experience with the new boy in the guest room left Jack feeling haunted. Something traumatic had happened to that boy, and he was not convinced that it all had to do with just one spell. If the new kid was the Warlocke, everyone was in trouble—although Jack had no idea why a Warlocke was coming in the first place.

He was sitting in the living room with Chase and Vidalia, who had heavy-sighed several times apiece. Jack was not about to go in for another magic lesson to liven the mood. He would rather have a few teeth extracted or a nose-ectomy.

"Let's go somewhere," he said suddenly, looking at Vidalia. At the confusion on her face, he asked, "Can't you pop us somewhere?"

"Me?"

"Well, yeah. Like you did to bring us here in the first place," Chase said.

"I didn't bring you here. My father did." She was horrified. "I can't do that."

"We saw you do it at my house." Jack disagreed.

"Well, yes, I did pop out of there—as you say—but that was just me, and it was only a few blocks away. Only my father has the kind of power to take so many people across the ocean itself, but he's arguably one of the most powerful wizards in centuries."

"Really?" Jack had assumed this was all normal for them.

"Well, yes. He's a very powerful wizard. And it's unusual that someone as young as myself can transposition at all. But I'm definitely not ready to transposition all of us somewhere—not even to another room."

"Oh." Chase looked at the floor and sighed again.

"Can't you fly brooms or a magic carpet or something?" Jack asked.

Vidalia laughed. "Well," she said, "perhaps there is one way I could take you around." Then she thought better of it. "Oh, but we shouldn't. It's dangerous out there for you."

Chase's face lit up. "Oh come on, Vidalia. I'm bored stiff. Let's go. What could it hurt?"

"Easy for you to say. You weren't turned into a parade of farm animals earlier." At that, Chase and Vidalia snickered.

"Well, what is the one way you had in mind?" Chase asked.

"Oh, I don't suppose it would hurt to show you."

Chapter Fifty-Six
A Violin?

———

Vidalia took them to a part of the house where the boys had never been. It was kind of like a garage, though she referred to it as the workshop.

There were no cars—the boys were looking. Above what appeared to be a workbench was a strange shelving unit with a score of square holes, similar to the kind hotels use for guest mail and messages. Vidalia reached up to one and removed a small blue helmet, about the size of a golf ball.

"Here it is. A stratovarious." She beamed.

The boys stared at it, neither with any idea how the little toy would help them in the least.

"A Stradivarius?" Chase asked. "That's not a Stradivarius. Those are worth a fortune and generally look a lot more like violins." Among his stranger habits, Chase had a thing for chamber music.

Vidalia sneered. "I didn't say it was a Stradivarius. I said it was a stratovarious."

The boys did not see what it mattered. Jack shrugged. "Ok."

Vidalia let out a heavy sigh and a growl of frustration. "Look."

She moved out to the middle of the workshop and placed it on the floor. "Oh, I know I'm going to regret this."

She waved her hand, releasing a shower of golden light, and instantly the little blue helmet became a large blue helmet that easily took up half the workshop. It looked a lot more like a shiny blue, metallic bubble with seats inside. "It was folded up—for storage. This is how it normally looks."

The boys had no idea what they were looking at, but at least this seemed to hold more promise than a toy.

"A stratovarious is a magic-imbued vehicle, mostly used for leisurely rides and such—entertainment. Bringing people places uses a lot of magical energy. This vehicle is warded for a lot of things—safety, speed and efficiency. So the operator has only to use a minimum of magic, but it's extremely safe and fast. It has various uses—it can fly, hover, go underwater and even go into space."

Now the boys looked at it with newfound respect. "Whoa," they said in unison.

"Let's go," Chase said eagerly, looking at Vidalia.

Vidalia was uncertain. She fidgeted about. "I don't know."

"Well, do you need a license or something?" Chase asked.

Jack added, "Did your dad say you couldn't drive it without him?"

"Well, no and no. But, uh, you," she pointed at Jack, "seem to have a way of getting into trouble. That's all I need is for something to happen. Besides, I don't think my dad wants you to leave the house. It's not safe."

"Come on. I'm going crazy staying bottled up in here. Let's go. You can take us around town or something, and we'll come right back."

"Well …"

"Come on, come on." Chase joined in.

"Argh. All right. I know I'm really going to regret this." She turned to the stratovarious and said, "Open."

Chapter Fifty-Seven
A Violin Ride

T he boys watched the doors glide open, obliging Vidalia's command. She waved them in.

"There are no seatbelts," Jack said as he sat down.

She smiled. "Try to stand up."

He did but got nowhere. It was as if the seat had glued him down, and not just his clothes. The harder he pulled, the harder the seat pulled back.

"That's cool, but I will be able to get out later, right?"

"Of course. It's a safety precaution. Say 'release' when you want out."

With that she closed the door, and the machine began to hover silently in the workshop. To the boys, it was strange to be in a machine that made no noise—being used to buses, cars and trains that made a great deal of it. In fact, if it was not for a small rising sensation in Jack's abdomen, he would never have known it was doing anything.

He was curious how she was going to get it out of the workshop. There was no overhead door since it was not a garage. For a second, he thought she was going to take it right through the ceiling when, all of a sudden, everything became gigantic.

Having had this experience several times earlier in the day, Jack knew right away what had happened, but Chase was unnerved. "Whoa! Everything is huge."

"It's ok, the strato shrank so we can get it out of the workshop," Vidalia said. "It also stays this size during flight to lessen the chances of being spotted by humans. If they see us, they think we're an odd-looking bird."

"Amen," Chase said, mumbling, but refused to repeat it when Vidalia asked him to.

The stratovarious maneuvered around items in the workshop—a leaning broom, a rake, a cat and a hanging bicycle that looked unlike any Jack had ever seen. The cat, which Jack had not yet seen in the house, did look very normal, except it was mammoth in their present, shrunken state.

Luckily, Vidalia was skilled enough to get around playful cats—the swipe it took at them was well avoided. They came to a small round portal in the wall, which opened as an aperture as soon as the stratovarious neared, and they were outside, flying in the open air.

The sunny morning was giving way to a cloudy October afternoon, but there were beams of sunlight punching through the clouds. As the stratovarious rose, their view of the vast countryside surrounding the little village of Bristelmestune, and the larger town of Brighton, broadened.

"This is awesome," Jack heard Chase repeating over and over.

Jack realized he was gripping the armrest so tightly that his knuckles were turning white. Several times he had to calm himself enough to relax his hands only to find that he was clenching them again a minute or two later.

The movement and turns the stratovarious made were effortless. They were handled by the machine in such a way that the sensation of turning was canceled by the tilt, so it hardly felt as if it was moving. Even more amazing was that it seemed Vidalia was not driving it, exactly, but that it was just going where she wanted it to, somehow. For the most part, she was as much a passenger as they.

They drifted back down toward an area more densely populated but still in Bristelmestune.

"Well, this is the town. There isn't much to see, really."

It was a nice-looking town, but it was just a town, with people milling about and little shops. Until Jack started reading some of the names of the shops, he thought it was the same as any other town.

One sign read, "Gizmos Galore," while another advertised "Doodads by the Dozen," and one shop was called "Servo Central."

"Is every shop in town only about electronics and gadgets and stuff?" Jack asked.

As Vidalia was about to answer, Chase asked, "What are you talking about? Do 'The Business Planner' and 'Banking by Banks' sound like electronics shops?" He motioned at the same signs Jack was looking at.

Vidalia cleared her throat. "Well, I think you're both forgetting that Bristelmestune is a town built on magic. So the shops—"

"Ohhhh, I get it," Chase said. "So they become shops that sell whatever it is you happen to be looking for."

"Exactly."

"That's too cool." He put his nose against the window again.

"C'mon, can't we go into Servo Central?" Jack pleaded.

"Or Bonds 'n' Munis?" Chase begged.

Vidalia shook her head. "You two are pathetic. What exactly do you do for fun?"

They looked at each other and shrugged. "Well, what are the stores called for you?" Jack asked.

"Never mind." Under her control, the stratovarious sped off again down the street. "Anyway, we can't get out of the strato. My dad would kill me. Right now, even people who grew up with magic probably won't notice another strato flying down the street, but if someone in the Society of All Magicks spots you directly, there is no telling what might happen."

"Oh, The Golden Crust. My favorite pizza shop." Chase gestured as they glided past a store that Jack saw as Power Packs Plus.

"We just ate lunch. You're hungry again?"

"I can't help it," he said sadly. "I have a high metabolism."

"Hey, what's with all the Halloween decorations? You guys go crazy for that stuff or what?" Jack had never seen so many Halloween decorations in a town.

"Yeah, I was thinking the same thing." Chase agreed.

"Well, Halloween is only a couple of days away," Vidalia said.

Jack counted days in his head and realized it was Sunday. "Oh, crap, that's right. We've got school tomorrow."

"No, silly. I just said Halloween is a couple of days away."

The boys both eyed her strangely, and Chase said, "So?"

"So. It's a holiday, you dork."

"Um," Jack started.

"No it's not," Chase finished.

"Halloween is always a ... Wait, you mean you don't get the week off for Halloween? Are you kidding me?"

Jack's eyes went wide. "Wait. You mean you do?"

Chase grabbed Jack's shoulder. "We seriously need to move here." He looked down the street. "I mean, look at all the pizza places they've got."

Jack did not get a chance to chuckle at that—the moment the words left Chase's mouth, the stratovarious shot off at a fast clip, jerking everyone's head back.

"What was that for?"

Vidalia looked around. "I didn't do that."

Chapter Fifty-Eight
Ricochet

———

T hey were going fast and seemed to be picking up speed. All three looked around trying to find some explanation, when Vidalia spotted it. "Look, it's another strato, and I think it's chasing us."

Out the back window, she pointed at a red speck in the distance. The speck was getting closer.

"The safety wards must have picked up on it and moved us to prevent a collision." They were climbing higher into the sky. "I don't know if I am powerful enough yet to get away from them."

Reluctantly she seemed to take control of the machine, but it was obvious she was struggling to come up with something to do. After a moment, resolve spread across her face, and the device started into a dive, aimed toward a thicket of trees. With a slight delay, the red stratovarious followed suit. They shot through the wood—weaving and dodging—zipping around heavy moss-laden tree trunks.

As they were trying to evade their pursuers, it occurred to Jack that they were probably looking for him. Surely they thought he was the Warlocke and would stop at nothing to get to him—even if it was at the expense of his friends.

I assure you, the line between our people and dark magic is not the only line they will cross, and cross gladly. Pesky's words from the night before rang through his head.

Also roaring through his head was the fact that he was not the Warlocke. He had no idea who was, but what if something happened during the chase and his friends got hurt. Why should they have to suffer, too? It was Jack those people wanted.

He made a decision. "Wait. I thought of something. Vidalia, stop the strato."

"Why?"

"Just do it."

In a small meadow—as quickly as it had rocketed off at top speed—the stratovarious slowed to a stop.

"Ok." He looked at Chase and Vidalia in turn. "Know it's for the best."

Before they could say a word, he rapidly said, "Release. Open."

Simultaneously his seat released him, the door swung open and the strato returned to normal size. As they watched this unfold in shock, he cast the Fyrelocke on the floor of the strato and jumped out, rolling onto the wooded ground. "Close," he said. "Now go home." As the door finished closing, he smacked the side of the machine—as if scaring off a horse. Obediently and without a sound, the stratovarious shrank and soared into the trees.

An instant later, the red stratovarious made an abrupt stop almost atop Jack. Tinted windows made it impossible to see who was inside, but he would not be kept in suspense for long.

The doors slid open without a sound.

Chapter Fifty-Nine
A Monstrous Good Time

T he two things that emerged from the red stratovarious were positively disgusting. Both were in the rough shape of a person—with legs, arms and a lump at the top that might be considered a head, but there the similarity ended.

The one closest to Jack was made up entirely of spiders—all swarming, surging and scurrying together in a bevy that made up the thing. It was easily three times the size of a normal man in thickness and produced a constant buzzing, a kind of scuttling sound.

The other was similar in size and shape but was definitely not made of spiders. It was hard to tell from where Jack was standing, but it seemed to be gelatinous green goo. He stared at it, trying to remember where he had seen that before, when it occurred to him what it was. Phlegm. Snot. Flowing, green, sticky, shiny snot.

Areas of the surface of this one were clear, while others were streaked with yellow and darker green colors. It jiggled as it moved and left a trail of slime everywhere it touched.

Watching the two freakish monsters unfold themselves from the stratovarious, he reconsidered. Being safely inside a nice blue stratovarious with his friends—even if it was being chased—seemed a better option than the one he now faced.

With his friends safely away, Jack realized there was no point in standing there. He turned on his heels and ran.

The snot-monster moved to chase him, but the creature's phlegm-feet stuck to the ground amazingly well, and it fell flat on its little lump head.

The spider-monster was able to pursue Jack without any sticky issues. Despite being a loosely bound blob of spiders, the thing moved surprisingly well. The spiders working in concert resembled pulsing muscles within the form of the larger beast, and before too long it was gaining on the boy.

Jack risked a glance behind him. The spider-thing was slowly picking up the distance between them, while the snot-thing was plodding along farther behind, falling over at intervals. Jack was not sure what to do, but he knew that any chance of outrunning the spider-thing was probably slim at best. Climbing a tree would be worse. Spiders could definitely climb trees.

He could only hope that the circuitous route through the trees would slowly knock individual spiders off the larger mass of the monster, making the thing smaller and smaller. Jack knew—the trees were almost taking entire chunks out of him as he leapt and dodged around them.

He had only one other idea—not a very good one, but it was all he had. He began to veer gently to the right, taking one small step to the right for every four or five he took. With any luck, maybe it would work. It had better work. He was starting to run out of steam, and who knew if spider-monster-things even had steam.

He kept veering to the right, hoping that he was not turning sharply enough to allow the snot-thing a chance to double back on him.

There it was. Through the trees, Jack saw the red stratovarious ahead. He had done it—making a large looping circle around the wood, back to the strato.

The spider-monster was getting closer, and Jack soon realized it had come close enough to cast blobs of bundled spiders at him. One zipped past his head, hitting a tree just as he sidestepped it. The loose spiders scattered, scuttling back into the forest around him.

He would have to make this quick.

Chapter Sixty
Close Call for a Whisper

Jack turned on his best, last burst of speed. It was not much—it was all he had left—but it was enough. He leapt headfirst into the red stratovarious only seconds ahead of the spider-demon. As soon as he was in the door, he said, "Close," and plopped into the driver's seat.

With the doors closed, spiders by the millions swarmed over the windows of the strato. Jack could only hope the thing was well made with no cracks and crevices.

The interior of the stratovarious had no steering wheel, no pedals, no knobs—nothing. He hoped that whoever sat in the driver's seat could control the thing.

Spiders swarmed the windows outside. Luckily, they had found no way in. Not yet.

Before they could, Jack wanted desperately to get the thing moving. He sat in the seat and pictured where he wanted to go.

Nothing.

He feared he was losing his chance. He could not possibly have much time left.

The spiders outside were like rain, pattering violently against the outer casing of the strato. Knowing they were out there, even with his eyes closed, he could not focus.

Breathing heavily from the sprint, he wiped sweaty hands on his pants, brushed the hair out of his eyes, and tried again.

He pictured Pesky's house the way it had looked after they had taken off. He made himself truly want to go there. He envisioned the stratovarious lifting from the ground, zipping off in that direction.

This time, it worked.

The stratovarious abruptly lifted and zoomed off through the trees. Whistling wind blew the windshield clean of spiders.

Jack flew briefly through a ray of golden sunlight, feeling light as a feather, and back out into the cloud-filled sky. He was able to see the fields around Bristelmestune, and his heart surged with joy.

Freedom.

It was positively exhilarating.

"That was thoroughly impressive." It was the oily voice of Gina Cankrot, hushed and coming from behind his left ear.

Chapter Sixty-One
The Truth That Isn't

Y es, quite." The thin, reedy voice of Kee Cankrot came from behind his right ear. "The way you overcame two of the most dreadful of monsters—without using any magic whatever—and here we were almost ready to believe you had no magic in you."

"Until we realized that's exactly what you want us to think," Gina said, as Jack turned around in his seat to face them. "Positively brilliant, but we're no fools."

Suddenly he realized the truth. He had not made the strato move. They had.

He could not believe it. They saw it as some ploy he had schemed to make them think he had no magic—this, even though he had no magic.

Right now, the stratovarious under their control was taking him wherever they had in mind to take him.

"Mom. Dad." Jack did his best to mimic his performance from the previous morning. He extended his arms openly and forced his lips into a relieved smile. "Thank goodness you made it. Did you see those things?"

They were not buying it. "Ah, ah, ah." Gina waved a finger at him. "No lying to the momma."

From the thrill of victory to crushing defeat in seconds. For less than a minute, he thought he had gotten the strato going—it had been breathtaking. For a brief moment, he thought he had made it.

Now, he understood it all. The Cankrots had set a trap. If he had gotten back to the stratovarious, they would be in it, waiting, invisible. If he had not, the monsters would have brought him back. Either way, they had him.

Now they thought he had cooked up a plan to hide his magic, so they would believe he was not the Warlocke. No matter that he was not the Warlocke and never thought he needed a plan to prove it.

He decided telling them that would do little good, so he sat back in his seat. Wherever they were going, he could do little about it now.

Chapter Sixty-Two
Your Mightiness

T hey must have cast some sort of sleeping spell on him. The next thing he knew, he was in a dark room, curled in a ball on the ground, in more pain than he could ever remember. He started to get up but had only gotten into a crouch when he felt a push on his shoulders.

"Stay on your knees." Gina's voice was hushed but commanding.

Not a problem. He was not the least bit sure that he still had knees. His body hurt everywhere.

Kee called loudly across the room. "Your Mightiness, the boy is awake."

Jack's response—a rebellious and resounding, "Who are you calling a boy?"—was lost in a whimper of pain that left his challenge garbled and pathetic. His head was pounding and felt like an anvil, but he lifted it and tried to get a peek at whoever was on the other side of the room. He could not see much.

The room was dark, lit only by a mild green glow that seemed to come from the stone walls themselves. Something stirred. Through bleary eyes Jack realized that, whatever it was, it was coming closer. Slowly.

It walked with a hitch. A scraping noise echoed off the walls with every step, a grinding that surely meant the thing was dragging one of its legs behind. "Your Mightiness" seemed to be lacking a little in the mighty department.

The thing came about halfway and stopped. Jack could not see much except a dark shadow, some distance away, in the glow of the green light.

"Warlocke?" The voice sounded ancient and feathery light, leaving the word to hang sourly in the air. The shadow sniffed the air as if it could smell prey. The scratchy, frail voice asked, "Oleagina? Caitiff? A Warlocke you say?"

It sniffed the air once more and began to walk again. "I think not." It spat the words out bitterly. Neither of the Cankrots said a word, but Jack could feel one of them shaking—whichever of them was on his left.

Chapter Sixty-Three
Blast It All

———

The shadowy figure came about three steps closer when a sudden thud stopped it short.

"Blast it all!" The aged voice cursed in a hiss. In the dim light, it was impossible to tell what had fallen.

"I truly need to get that fixed," the frail voice said grimly as it stooped to pick up whatever had fallen. It was only then that Jack caught enough in the dim light to gather what it was—the thing's own arm.

In confirmation, the figure jammed the arm back on, which made crunchy, goopy, smooshing sounds. It began walking again. By then, it was clearly a human form wearing a dark hooded robe. When it got to about ten paces, it stopped and lowered the hood, revealing the wrinkled, leathery head of an aged and battered man.

"As I was saying—Yes." The withered voice spoke with eerie softness. "A Warlocke, Oleagina? Caitiff?"

"Your Mightiness," the two said at the same time, their words riddled with fear.

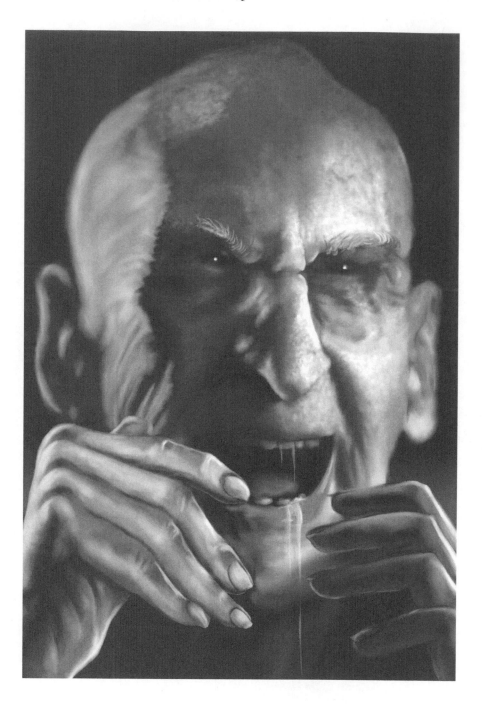

"I think not!" He shouted the words and raised his head a little. When he did, his lower jaw snapped and hung down slack, as on broken hinges. It swung loosely back and forth. A small drop of spittle dribbled, leaving a trailer that spanned from his mouth to the floor.

Jack was a little surprised that Kee and Gina were so afraid. This one seemed like he could be taken down fairly easily—all you had to do was rush him and he would fall to pieces, literally.

The figure tried to say something that came out garbled, so he reached up to right his slackening jaw. Once he had it on properly, he cursed again. "Blast it. Blast it, I say!"

He looked sharply at the two Cankrots assembled before him and at Jack, still on his knees. "I do not think this one is the Warlocke, but we will test him nonetheless. For your sake, I hope he is." He licked his lips, a snake scenting the air. "For what it's worth, the boy himself believes he is not the Warlocke." Another sniff. "Gina? Do you know who he thinks the Warlocke is?"

"No, Mighty Wargothe."

"Newt." He burst out laughing, a dry, rusty laugh—the sound of dead leaves raked into a pile. "Newt," he said a second time as a mumble.

Nobody else made a sound.

Newt? Who the heck is Newt?

When he had finished laughing in that reptilian way, the Wargothe licked his lips and looked at the boy. "Magic or no, I understand you fancy yourself terribly clever. Do you, Boomershine?"

Probably not one of those questions that should get an answer, Jack remained silent.

"You got away from my bees once but not a second time. Did you, Boomershine?" He scowled at Oleagina and Caitiff. "Not that getting away from my bees is always as difficult as it ought to be."

He sneered at the Cankrots a final time and spoke softly. "Now, dally no more and get the Warlocke." He turned to walk away and suddenly twisted back. "Ah. The Fyrelocke, if you would." He extended his hand out to Caitiff, who was closer. "I trust you have at least recovered the Fyrelocke."

Jack could feel both the Cankrots begin to tremble.

"Oh, Wargothe," Gina said.

"The boy had no fyrestone on his person." Caitiff interrupted her with a small flicker of nobility.

A lazy wave of the Wargothe's hand sent ugly green sparks into the air. Caitiff Cankrot was blasted bodily back against the hard stone wall behind him, making only a hollow thunk as he hit the wall.

Oleagina shivered.

The withered, ancient man stared at her, fury in his eyes. "Throw the boy downstairs then. For now." He began to walk away but stopped and added, with his back to them, "And Oleagina, please do see that you lock the door this time, would you?" He asked, thick with sarcasm.

Left unspoken in the air was what would happen if she were to forget.

Chapter Sixty-Four
The Amphibious Bedroom

A fter she had attended to Kee, who seemed to be no worse than unconscious, Gina took Jack through a hallway and down a long flight of stairs.

The cellar, also lined with stone walls, had a vaguely moldy smell, and was dark and dank besides. All in all, not the kind of place you want to be thrown.

Mrs. Cankrot followed behind Jack, pushing his back every few seconds to shepherd him in the direction she wanted him to go.

He considered trying his Mommy-dearest routine but decided it probably would not work. Based on the reaction it got in the stratovarious, he considered it unlikely the Cankrots had ever really fallen for it, but judged it easier to humor Jack than call him on it. Had he not gotten out before they came back, the gambit probably would have paid off for them.

They came to a doorway, and Mrs. Cankrot stepped in front of him to open the door. She flicked her fingers abruptly, and there was light in the room. No shower of golden sparks—just light.

She gave him another light push in the back, and he stumbled into the room.

There was not much to see. It was a small room—smaller even than his bedroom at home—white walls, yellowed with age, and stained with prints and smudges. A bed was on the left, a twin-size with a single mattress on a spring. It was bare, with no pillow, blankets, bed sheets or other linens. There was one small window at the top of the facing wall, and nothing else in the room.

Jack was struck by something as he surveyed the layout. The strange young man who had been brought to Pesky had made a double of this room with the room he had been given—even down to the hole in the curtains. That hole perfectly matched the small window in this room. The position of the bed, the starkness, the lack of decoration—it looked exactly as the room had after the young man had *improved* it.

Jack felt a shiver.

Could Newt, to which the Wargothe had referred, be a boy who had lived here in this room? Could that same boy be the young man now staying with the Dorfnutters?

Gina, unaware of Jack's epiphany, was all business. "The entire room is warded," she said. To demonstrate, she struck her finger against the wall, which answered with a deluge of green sparks. The walls all around the room lit up. Every wall was protected.

She plucked her finger back and stuck it in her mouth.

Got it. Touching the wall—bad. Don't touch the wall.

She said nothing more but emitted a small harrumph and stepped out the door, slamming it behind her. A moment later, the door, the frame and the knob all lit briefly with a green glow as well.

So much for the idea that she would forget to lock the door.

Chapter Sixty-Five

Just Enough for Air

It occurred to Jack that when he had heard the old man goad her about locking the door, he had thought the Wargothe was referring to Jack's escape from his own house during their watch. But could the scraggly old man have meant that the boy, Newt, had gotten out on his own somehow?

Jack thought that was unlikely. *What was that spell that Pesky said the kid got hit with? Cogni-pinkus humungous? Something like that.*

Jack looked around the room again. Definitely not a cozy place to kick back, relax or play some video games in. One look at the room left him with several thoughts—leisure and comfort were not high on the list. A hospital room would have been luxurious in comparison.

He decided that it could not hurt to try the obvious. After all, what if she really had forgotten to lock the door? True, he had seen it all turn green, but what if he spent weeks in here only to find that the green glow he had seen around the doorknob meant she had accidentally unlocked it? He would be kicking himself for not having at least tried the doorknob. It was worth trying.

Despite that, the image of Oleagina sucking her finger after touching the wall, and the shower of ugly green sparks it sent flying, left him pause. What if touching the wall would knock him unconscious? Maybe she had been somewhat immune to it, but he would get knocked on his ... well, knocked on the floor. He did not want to find out the hard way that those sparks packed more punch than she had let on.

He took out his wallet and prodded the doorknob with it. A flurry of green sparks shot out. Any thought of trying it with his bare hand went fleeting. It was so strong, the surge of power made his hair stand on end.

If only he had a bit of Vidalia's magic. Maybe he could use that somehow, but then he realized that these people had dark magic. In all likelihood, that would trump anything Vidalia could do. She would be as trapped in here as he.

He turned and looked at the window.

Mrs. Cankrot had not done anything to that. Perhaps there was no ward on it. Maybe, just maybe, that was a way out.

Standing on the bed, trying not to touch the wall, he ventured a go at the window.

This time, he could not get close enough to prod it with his wallet before the green sparks plumed. When his wallet aligned with the wall, even before getting to the sunken part, sparks flew.

Ok. Back to the door.

He studied it for a minute and realized there was a small gap beneath the door for the threshold. Despite the impossible—that he could slip through that gap—he was curious.

He decided to see if that gap was closed off, too. He opened his wallet to see what might work—his school ID card. Perfect.

Bending at the door, careful not to touch the door itself, he inserted the card into the gap. No green sparks. No warning bells. No resistance.

Interesting.

He was not sure what that proved, but it was something.

Chapter Sixty-Six
Your Fate Hinges on This

———

Jack sat down on the bed, springs squeaking, to consider the door a little longer. He realized it was a normal interior door—except for the cosmic ward of protection on it. Aside from that, it was normal. And as most interior doors do, this one had the hinges on the inside of the room.

Could it be?

As before, it was unlikely, but maybe they had forgotten to extend the ward of protection to the hinges themselves. If so, that might be a way out. It could not hurt to try.

He touched his wallet to the hinge that was at eye level. No sparks.

Could it be?

It seemed so obvious to him, but these were people who were used to relying on magic. Maybe they would never consider the possibility of removing the hinges, which would be as good as unlocking the door.

Could they be removed? That was the question. Jack had experience in removing hinges once when he was trying to get one of his creations out of his room. It was too large—by an inch or two—

to fit through the door. Even with tools, it had not been as easy as he had expected.

And he had no tools now.

And he had no magic—ever.

First, though, he had another problem. Removing hinges was not exactly a quiet business. That might be a problem before he got very far.

Would they be listening for noises? He pictured Oleagina waiting outside the door, guarding it. He placed his palm on the wallet and smacked it against the door a couple of times. Green sparks sailed into the air—the booming echoed down the hall.

He listened for a response.

Nothing.

He tried again.

Still nothing.

Good. Gina must have gone off to deal with other stuff, Jack thought acidly. *Burning ants with a magnifying glass, kicking the neighborhood dog or stealing the left wheels off wheelchairs. That sort of thing.*

Wherever she was, it suited Jack fine. As long as it was not here.

Another look at the hinges confirmed his thoughts—prying hinge pins out is nearly impossible with bare fingers. He looked in his wallet for something that might help, something thin but strong. None of his cards would be strong enough to get a hinge pin moving. They would just crack.

He cursed himself for not having his keys or pocketknife with him. Either would have been perfect for this—better than an ID card, anyway.

Not much else in the room but the bed—and the springs.

That gave him an idea.

He hefted the mattress—grimy, worn and matted as it was—off the bed and looked at the spring set beneath it.

Bingo!

Where the springs connected to the posts were four reasonably thin metal plates. Would they be thin enough? Could he get one off without tools?

He began checking each one. The third had screws loose enough to remove by hand. After a minute or two, he was able to separate the connecting plate from the bedpost.

Scrambling to the door excitedly, Jack fumbled with it in the middle hinge, trying his best not to accidentally scrape the door for the flurry of green sparks that would cause. He tried not to get his hopes up. After all, the hinges could be warded in a different way—such as a ward that makes them never come out. Or maybe he could get the hinges out, but it would do no good because the ward on the door would keep it sealed. Even if this succeeded, it did not mean the plan would actually work.

He tried the steel plate between the hinge and the hinge pin. Tight, but it looked like it might work well enough.

Whew.

Now, all he needed was leverage enough to get the pin out. At the moment, it would not budge.

Using his shoe for a hammer, he was able to get the middle pin out and quickly followed with the other two, scraping the door only twice with the connecting plate. Luckily, his hand never made contact. Green sparks flew into his face but otherwise did nothing.

Jumpy but giddy, he could almost taste freedom. He knew that getting the door open was unlikely if the ward on the frame kept the door sealed. Or worse, if he did get the door open and Gina Cankrot was standing there when he did. The hinges would be no option a second time.

"Well." He took a deep breath and said to no one, "Here goes nothing."

With his shoes off, he positioned his toes under the gap of the door, cringing, waiting for the shower of sparks his toes might set off in touching the underside of the door.

No sparks.

With his toes, he lifted the door a little and felt it loosen in the frame. Then, using the steel plate from the bed like a pry bar, he pulled the hinged side free of the frame.

When it came off in his hands—with no sparks—he wanted to jump for joy.

In the hallway outside the room, there was nobody waiting for him. No Gina. No Caitiff. No Wargothe.

Excellent.

For a second, he considered trying to put the door back in the frame to maintain the ruse, but he knew it would waste valuable escape time. He did lean the door back in but left it at that. It would not fool anyone who gave it more than a passing glance, but maybe that would be all he needed to get away.

After that, it was easy.

Apparently they never expected him to get out of the room, as the first casement window he found outside the room was not warded, at least not from the inside. Other than finding something on which to stand, he was able to get out of the house without incident.

Chapter Sixty-Seven
To the Eternal Home

I t was well into dusk as Jack scurried from the house.

After getting out, he was so pumped on adrenaline that he did not think to look back to remember where it was or get some bearing on where he might be. Not that in the semi-darkness he would have seen much anyway. He just ran.

The house must have been on the outskirts of Bristelmestune, surrounded by a small wood where no other houses were visible. He was fumbling his way through trees and bramble, hoping he was going roughly in the direction of the town but not caring much, as long as it put distance between him and the house.

His breath was visible in bursts of steam as he fumbled around in the cold, darkening air.

That was rather impressive, young Boomershine.

Jack stopped in his tracks.

Wow. Now that was impressive, too. I've never seen anyone freeze stock-still and jump about a foot in the air, and both at the same time. Bravo!

"Trygg," Jack said, searching around.

The puriform's nose and ears nudged up through some bramble, and its eyes peeked out, looking brightly at Jack.

"Hey, you couldn't have come a bit sooner?"

When would have been a good fit for your busy social schedule? Trygg's expressive ears moved low to the sides.

"I mean, like fifteen or twenty minutes sooner? Or maybe like when I got caught?"

Oh, that. The ears sloped back confidently along the puriform's head. *Why would I have come sooner? Get-togethers can be so boring. I mean they go on and on—people droning on about their arms popping off at intervals and such. It's all so tiresome.*

"Well, you could've helped me."

Young Jack. Why in heaven would I do that? You did fine on your own, didn't you? You are here now, all in one piece. You did well. As I said before, rather impressive indeed.

The puriform abruptly changed the subject. *You like the ocean?*

"Um. Sure. I guess so," Jack said, bemused. "Why?"

Only about a hundred paces or so in the direction you're going and you would have had a nice long drink of it. The puriform lifted a nose and sniffed the air. *Though, a bath might do you a spot of good. Never mind that. As I was saying, navigation is certainly not your strong suit, and now seemed a more apt time and use for the aid only I could provide.*

"Um. Well, uh, which way should I go then?"

The ears went straight up. *How about this way?*

In a blink, they were standing in a cemetery. Evening was upon them now. It was getting hard to see and, with the cold damp air, a low fog was clinging to the ground.

Chapter Sixty-Eight
Funerary Toying

Y ou know, Trygg, I think I may have liked the ocean better.
It's strange, the places where you think I belong."

Oh, come now. We'll only be here a moment or two, and then I'll
have you home in a jiff. Besides, I am—once again—about to save you from
hours of toil and drudgery.

"What exactly would I have been doing during those hours of toil
and drudgery?"

Why, digging up this grave, naturally. Trygg smiled expansively—all
too glad Jack had taken the bait—while grandly waving a hand
toward the grave at their feet.

Jack stared at it in disbelief. He had not expected that.

"Um. And why exactly would I do that?"

Why, Jack, here I thought you so observant. Have you not yet noticed whose
grave at which we stand?

Jack turned to look at the grave marker, but the light was so poor
he could not make anything out. He stepped closer to it, intrigued,
but had to get within a few feet in order to read it.

Here lies the treasured son
of Jonathon and Emily.

Christopher James Locke

So little.
So little time among us.

The saddest thing about the gravestone was that there was only the one year—the baby had died as an infant.

"Trygg, I already know that Christopher Locke is not buried there. There was a switch. Another child died in the accident. I already know all about it."

Ah, excellent. Then you know who that baby was? The ears went straight up again—attentive.

"Uh. Well." Jack stammered. "Um, not exactly. I thought for a while it was the real Jack Boomershine."

Oh, I thought you were the real Jack Boomershine. The ears slowly spread down, relaxed—slyly giving the impression that the puriform was confused.

Jack knew the puriform was anything but confused. "Really, Trygg? I don't want to have to look at this."

Seeing is believing. Trust me on this. Oh, which reminds me, you might want to get the Fyrelocke out for this. You'll need it.

Jack reflexively checked his pocket before realizing he had tossed it into the strato before he jumped out—not wanting it to be taken when he was captured.

Don't worry. I have it right here. The puriform smiled craftily, then pitched it to Jack, who caught it one-handed. *From now on, don't leave home without it. Ok?*

"How did you get it?"

I know. I'm so strikingly good-looking and devilishly charming that it's sometimes easy to forget I am a master of magic as well. The puriform blew lightly on its nails before polishing them against its furry chest. *But I am, you know.*

Since you've brought up dereliction of duty, how are you coming along sifting through all that paperwork we picked up this morning?

"Uh. I brought up what?"

Never mind, but how are you coming along with it?

"Well, we found my birth card and the one for Christopher Locke," Jack said. At the mention of the Locke baby, he pointed solemnly toward the grave.

Superb. The puriform smiled.

After a pause where Trygg seemed to be waiting expectantly for something, the puriform added, *Please do go on.*

"Well, that's pretty much it. Those cards are why I thought I was Christopher Locke, and he was the real Jack Boomershine. Madame Puffin cleared that up for me."

The puriform's face saddened, and its ears withered to the sides of its head. *Ah. I see, but ... eh, that's as far as you've gotten? Oh, my dear boy, you will have to do better. You must surely realize that every stitch of paper I gave you was done so of necessity. I supplied nothing that is irrelevant. Each and every paper there was given you for some reason. You must pore over every one with the diligence of an enthusiast—nay, a researcher—a scientist with the very lives of your patients hanging in the balance. For Jack, my friend, I tell you not lightly, lives do hang in the balance.*

"Oh." He let out a heavy sigh. Suddenly filled with guilt, he fumbled to change the subject. "Ok. I've got the Fyrelocke. Now what?"

No sooner had he said the words than the dirt surrounding the grave became invisible, revealing a coffin. Then the coffin itself became invisible, revealing a small bundle of bones.

Jack thought he was going to be sick, but Trygg's voice appeared in his head, as always. *Ah-ah-ah. No need to get sick, Jack. Take a closer look. Trust me.*

Intrigued, Jack did look closer. He tightened his grip on the Fyrelocke and took two small steps toward the hole, and then saw it. The little bundle of bones was nothing more than a child's toy, tinged—ever so faintly—with the green glow Jack had begun to associate with dark magic.

Otherwise, it was empty. There was no body in the grave.

Chapter Sixty-Nine
A Caustic Return

W hat does that mean?" Jack asked before realizing he was standing alone in the spare room at the Dorfnutter house.

He growled at the empty room. The little puriform had done it again. Twice in one day Trygg had "saved him from hours of toil and drudgery" without any explanation as to what it was the puriform was actually giving him.

It was clear that there was no body in the grave of Christopher Locke, but why would that matter? He already knew that the babies were switched at birth, and the real Christopher Locke must still be out there. In fact, he knew from Madame Puffin that the Warlocke was out there somewhere, which had to be Christopher Locke, right?

Jack shook his head, jammed the Fyrelocke into his pocket, and left the room in search of someone to tell that he was back safely.

He found Madame Puffin and Chase in the living room—Puffin reading a strange-looking book with animated frogs crawling from the cover image, and Chase pacing nervously back and forth.

"Jack!" Chase saw him first and came running at him. "What happened? How did you get here? You didn't die, did you?" Chase ripped off the questions so fast that Jack barely heard them. "Ah, skip that last one. Unless you're a zombie. You're not a zombie. Are you?"

Madame Puffin very sedately folded her book shut and set it on the table. She sat back on the couch and eyed Jack sharply.

"I know, I know. I shouldn't have done it, but I didn't want to risk having Vidalia and Chase get captured, too. It was me they were after." He defended himself against the stare she gave him. "Why should they get hurt because those whackos were after me?"

"Were you captured?" She asked rhymelessly—it must have been short enough.

"Yeah. They took me to see the Wargothe, who said I wasn't the Warlocke."

"And they let you go?"

"Well, uh, no. I kind of got away."

"Most remarkable," Puffin said in a staid tone but with a smirk. On the subject she said nothing further. "Now, very well, go get cleaned and we'll get you some small food. Later, we will discuss the trouble you've brewed, and on which all day long I have stewed. So for now, perhaps it is your turn on these events to brood."

"Whoa, she must be mad. That's four rhymes in a row against the same word," Chase said, not helping matters.

Puffin turned her caustic stare on Chase briefly before continuing. "In the meantime, I must try and notify Pescipalius and Vidalia of your return, who are now—this minute—searching for you at every turn."

Chapter Seventy
A Puffin Hat Trick

T he boys returned to the room, where Jack filled Chase in on far more details than he had given Puffin. For some reason, he could not bring himself to trust her or the Dorfnutters completely. Not that they had given any reason to distrust them, but they were not giving him all the information they had, either. Undeniably, there was more they knew than they were telling. Puffin was the midwife at the births of both Christopher Locke and Jack, and she had written the *Prophecy Untold* herself. Yet she had mentioned neither of these facts to Jack. What other things was she not telling him?

When he filled Chase in on the escape, his friend was in awe, but Jack knew it was nothing special. Anyone could have done it— pulling hinge pins was not exactly high technology.

He kept nervously putting the Fyrelocke on the end table and picking it back up again as he told Chase about the second run-in with Trygg. Chase was offended that the "bunny" seemed to be trying to avoid him, but Jack explained that it may have as much to do with his insistence on calling the puriform a "bunny" in the first place.

"Anyway, it probably has nothing to do with avoiding you. It is just that Trygg comes when it's convenient." He could not help adding, "And it happens to be convenient when you're not around."

Chase took offense, only half pretense.

Changing subjects, Jack told him about how he had been scolded for not going through the stack of papers. *For Jack, my friend, I tell you not lightly, lives do hang in the balance.*

Chase opened the closet doors and noticed immediately that the papers had been rearranged. "Well, you must have had time to go through them at some point."

"Whad'ya mean?" Jack hopped up from the bed.

He saw it, too. The stack had been organized differently when they last saw it. Instead of the two birth cards they had found earlier, sitting on top of the stack was a third.

"I haven't been back in here since this morning."

"Well, I guess ol' Trygg wanted you to find this one quickly."

Baby Girl Dorfnutter

Born:	13 December, 11:09AM
Weight:	7 lbs., 8 oz.
Length:	19 in.
Mother:	Molly S. Dorfnutter (nee Krebbs)
Father:	Pescipalius Perfidius Dorfnutter
Midwife:	Mme. T.B. Puffin

As before, the baby's name was handwritten at the bottom of the card: Vidalia Allium Dorfnutter.

Chase whistled. "Must've been a busy morning for Madame Puffin."

Jack had to agree. Midwife to three births?

He compared the three cards. Three babies, all born within five hours of one another at the same hospital, to the same midwife, and they all had the same weight and length. That was weird.

Vidalia? The stray thought popped into his head, and Jack had to think it through. *Well, that might make sense. It might explain why Puffin hangs around with the Dorfnutters so much.*

"Huh." He mumbled the word to himself as he reasoned it out further. *Could it possibly be? Could she be the Warlocke?*

"Why not?" he said—also to himself.

"Why not what?" Chase seemed to think Jack was talking to someone else. He turned to look behind but found nobody.

When he faced back, Jack looked him in the eye and said, "Maybe Vidalia is the Warlocke."

Chapter Seventy-One
Forecast: Foggy but Clearing

T hat can't be," Chase said.

"Well, why not? Vidalia said herself that there are no gender-specific roles in magic. She could be the Warlocke the same as anybody else."

"I'm not talking about that. I mean the prophecy says 'him.' You know, 'Swap *him* to the unfamiliar bed.'"

"Oh, I get it." Jack sat down and—from the end table—picked up the Fyrelocke again, thinking. "Well, it doesn't say the 'him' is the Warlocke. The 'him' might be the other kid." Jack's mouth opened wide. "Newt."

"What?" Chase looked baffled again and, just to be sure, took a look behind. Again, there was nobody there. "You really need to stop doing that," he said, turning back to Jack.

"No, I forgot to tell you about Newt."

"What's a newt?"

"Not a newt. Just Newt," Jack said. "While I was at the Wargothe's house—"

"Just Newt?" Chase asked. "What is that? Like, a skin cream or something? Cure zits lickety-split?" He paused for a second, scrunched his face, and said, "Ew, remind me never to say 'zits' and 'lickety' in the same sentence again. Bad image, bad image."

Jack gave up being patient and talked right over him. "Listen, would you? While I was there, the Wargothe said I thought the Warlocke was 'Newt'—as if he could see the picture of the kid in my head. He was reading my mind or something. And he thought that was hilarious. I was trying to figure out what he was talking about. And the only thing I can think of happened right before we left to go on the strato. I was thinking about the strange kid, and I was thinking he might be the Warlocke."

"Ok? So you think the strange kid is named Newt?" Chase thought about that for a second. "Well, it's a strange name, but kinda fits. Yeah. Strange kid, strange name. I'm thinking that works." He nodded in affirmation.

"No, I think the strange kid is … I mean, yes, I think he's named Newt, but I think he's the 'him' in the prophecy."

"What? He's the Warlocke?"

"No. The Wargothe knew Newt wasn't the Warlocke. I don't know how, but I mean, what if Vidalia is the Warlocke, and Newt is Pesky's real kid?"

Chase finally got it. "Holy cow."

"Yeah, and what if Puffin switched them." Jack was suddenly energized. "Wait. That's it. It all makes sense now."

He took a couple of deep breaths to pin it down in his own head.

"Three babies were born, first me—who happened to be born there. I still have to find out what that's about. Then the Locke baby—Vidalia. Finally the Dorfnutter baby—the kid we know now as Newt. Puffin switched them, and the Society of All Magicks somehow captured Newt, who they thought was Christopher Locke but was really Pesky's son." He was speaking animatedly—waving his arms and shooting his words out rapidly.

"Meanwhile, Vidalia goes on as Pesky's daughter, but she's really 'Baby Girl Locke.' Puffin is the midwife, so she has no problem switching the babies before the birth cards got made, or maybe she changed them after. Either way, not hard for her to do if she's the midwife." Jack took a deep breath. "After capturing Newt, the Society of All Magicks people do something about the car crash—I don't know what that is. They charm a doll to make the Brighton City police—non-magical police, who would never think about magic being used—into seeing a dead baby. The doll-baby gets buried, and the Society people pick the name Newt to give to the Locke baby to keep him under wraps. He gets kept in this creepy room at the Wargothe's house."

"Whoa," Chase said again.

"I know, creepy is a nice way to put it. Anyway, it all sounds so far-fetched, but I think it's right. Or mostly right." Jack took another deep breath.

"No, I mean, whoa, how the heck did you figure all that out? I'm only following you at about half-speed."

Without answering, Jack's eyes went distant, and he said in a murmur, "Oh crap."

"Now what?"

His eyes were wide. With one hand he held the Fyrelocke; with the other he pointed to the cards that were laid on top of the bed. His eyes got wider, and he pointed to the stack of papers on the floor of the closet.

"What?"

"There's green glow all over those papers. I don't think Trygg laid them out for us. Aw, jeez. I think someone in the Society of All Magicks found them."

He had not been holding the Fyrelocke when they first opened the closet doors. Now that he held it, the glow was clearly visible. The birth cards had it, the copy of the prophecy they had recreated from memory had it, and a good number of the other loose papers did, too.

"Which means …" Chase started.

"Which means, they know what we know," Jack finished. "They know that Vidalia is the Warlocke. Not me."

Jack held up the Fyrelocke in Chase's view. It was left unsaid between them, but they both knew it—the Warlocke was supposed to have the Fyrelocke, but did not.

After all, Jack was holding it.

Chapter Seventy-Two
An Abduction Production

Jack looked at Puffin, nervously pacing the living room, not as sedate as she had been earlier when she had known he would be coming back. Something had happened that was unexpected, her confidence broken.

"Vidalia is the Warlocke," he said loudly, to get her attention.

Chase stood at his side.

She stopped her pacing, turned to face them and smiled sadly. "Ah, Jack, ever so clever you are. I knew you would come through—but I fear you may be too late, although I hope that won't be the least bit true."

"Too late for what?" Chase had to ask.

She sighed miserably. "I can't seem to reach Vidalia or Pesky. I have no idea where they are, but my messages return unviewed—whether I send them near or far."

"What?" Jack asked. He knew this had to do with the evil, robed man he had seen earlier in the night. "The Wargothe has them," he said with bitter conviction.

Puffin frowned. "I cannot keep it from you—that is certainly my fear. Yet I know not what to do in help of those most dear."

"Take us up in the stratovarious. I bet I can find the Wargothe's house. I'm sure that's where they'd be."

"Oh no. Not that again. Jack, we are not even sure that's true." Her eyes lit with excitement. "I know. We shall call Mr. Dodder and Mr. Wimple. They will know what to do."

She set to calling them, which involved the magic vellum Jack and Chase had seen in Puffin's store.

Within minutes of sending the vellum, the two elderly men were standing in the living room, listening to Puffin recount how she had tried to get in touch with Pesky and Vidalia, to no avail.

"Well, Bea. I think you …" Mr. Dodder began.

"… made the right decision, indeed." Mr. Wimple finished for him.

Although Chase and Jack had heard their voices, this was the first time they were seeing the two elderly men. The men had to be in their eighties. Mr. Dodder was tall, with a shiny, bald pate and a thin mustache, while Mr. Wimple was short and stocky. Both wore tweed suits, and neither moved terribly quickly but instead limped and staggered along on thin rickety legs.

They seemed kindly men, smiling often, hugging Madame Puffin and placing their hands on Jack or Chase's shoulder in reassurance.

"No, I think it best …" Dodder said agreeably.

"… that everyone stay here for safety's sake …" Wimple continued the thought.

Dodder resumed, "… while Mr. Wimple and I see if we cannot locate …"

"… Pescipalius and Vidalia," Wimple finished for him. "Mr. Boomershine, I am most impressed you were able to get away. And you say …"

"… that you were able to get out only because Oleagina Cankrot …"

"... had forgotten to use magic on the hinges?"

"Most amazing," said Dodder.

"Astonishing," added Wimple. "Well, we had known for years ..."

"... that the Cankrots were involved in nefarious deeds ..."

"... but we have never been able to pin them down on anything ..."

"... quite so specific. This is excellent. Now, with this ..."

"... perhaps there will be enough to finally apprehend them ..."

"... and have it hold up well enough in the courts," finished Dodder, beaming and placing his hand on Jack's shoulder once again.

Jack could not help noticing that the man's thin mustache was the picture of precision, yet he had a small patch of stubble on his cheek that he had missed entirely.

Chapter Seventy-Three
Brighton Tourism Declines

———

The two men left abruptly not long after. They had one minor disagreement between them before leaving—over who should exit the door first. So it was mostly an uneventful meeting with them.

After returning to their room, Chase mentioned that he had secretly hoped the argument would sour and at least one of them would kick the other in the shins.

"Chase." Jack waved him off. "They're like a thousand years old."

"I know. It would have been hilarious."

Jack shook his head.

"What now?" Chase flopped on his bed and lazily propped his head up with a pillow.

"Well, there's still those papers." Jack gazed in the direction of the closet. "Want to help me look through them?"

"When you say 'want to,' what exactly do you mean?"

"You gonna help or not?"

They went through the stack—page after page—not reading each, but trying to get an idea of what the stack of papers as a whole might mean. Jack got so sick of seeing the green glow that he had to set the Fyrelocke down so he could see what he was doing.

They saw so many pages that were similar to one another that Chase came up with the idea to stack them in piles based on similarity. Being into finance, he called each stack a ledger. Jack let him call them whatever he wanted so long as he was helping.

By the end of it, aside from the three birth cards they had found previously, they had three "ledgers"—one with death certificates, one with patient records, and one with pages and pages of notes that the boys did not understand. The notes were written by doctors, and some were so old they were crumbling at the edges.

"You know, I think I see a pattern," Jack said after he had reviewed his seven millionth death certificate.

"Yeah." Chase agreed miserably. "They're all rectangular and have teeny black writing."

"No, really, almost every one of these death certificates began with a sudden coma from out of nowhere one to two weeks before death."

"Really? So if I understand you right, all these death certificates mean someone died, each and every time?"

"Chase, cut it out. I'm serious." Jack let out a huff. "I'm trying to figure out why Trygg thought I needed to see these."

After going through the second ledger—the pile of papers dealing with patient records—it became apparent that there was a trend for those as well. Almost all of them had to do with the sudden onset of schizophrenic or bipolar disorders. The people in these cases sometimes went on to live long lives afterward, but none were ever fully cured.

The boys tried to see if some of the people in the second set were also victims in the first set, hoping to spot a link between the two. None were.

Finally, they set into the doctor's notes. This was the hardest of the three ledgers to look at. Unlike the other two stacks, which were mostly standard-format forms, this last was all free-form notes and was compiled from different doctors over several years—some were centuries old.

One in particular caught Jack's interest.

Overall, I find the incidence of sudden-onset comas in the Brighton region is far higher than anywhere else in the world, higher even than in surrounding townes.

The sentence struck a chord with Jack, and he knew it was significant. He pulled the loose sheet from the stack and held it separately, reading the yellowed page further.

The doctor went on to speculate about possible causes that may be the root of the problem—water conditions, mills, wells, pollutants—but he was never able to identify anything conclusive.

As they pored over the stacks of paper, the boys found similar notes from other doctors indicating that either the rate of comas was dramatically higher in or around Brighton, or that statistical rates for symptoms of schizophrenia or dementia were. Whatever the cause, this increased rate of diagnosis had been happening for a long time.

Chapter Seventy-Four
The Theory of Everything

———

Finally, Jack came to the bottom of the stack. Chase had long since passed out on his bed. All that was left was a page torn from a book. Neither of the boys had noticed it before. They must have put it in the doctor's notes pile only because it did not fit with the formulaic papers in the other two piles. It looked like a pen-and-ink drawing or a woodcut that was very old.

The image showed three boys, not much older than Jack or Chase. Jack immediately recognized the three from his journey with Ignatius the night before. The caption beneath the woodcut read, "The Warlockes: Ignatius Locke, Ephraim 'the Dark' Locke and Aaron James Cross."

On the back of the page was another pen-and-ink drawing of an older man, probably in his fifties, who was oddly familiar. The caption read, "Father of all modern magicks: Aaron James Cross." No wonder the face was familiar. He had seen that man as a boy.

Yet something kept vexing him.

On the verge of figuring it out, he could feel all the pieces coming together, but the solution to the puzzle was not yet there. He was close. He might have all the right pieces—but they had to fit together correctly.

He looked at the three piles and replayed the facts in his mind.

"Man, that guy looks familiar," he said to himself as he looked at the older image of Cross, unable to put his finger on it.

Jack picked up the Fyrelocke to see if the feel of the rock might help him think. The remark he had made to Chase—after Dodder and Wimple left—popped back into his head. *Chase, they're like a thousand years old.*

As fast as the flash of light that announces the arrival of Pescipalius or Puffin, Jack had it.

He jumped up to wake Chase.

"I've got it. I've got it."

"Whatever it is, does it come with dipping sauces?" Chase asked, half asleep, before recognizing the excitement in Jack's eyes. "All right, what?" he asked, always fiery when he was hungry.

"Chase, I figured it out. I've got it." He punctuated each word with a shake of Chase's shoulders. "I think I understand everything."

Chase had to wake up a bit before Jack could get him to understand whole sentences. Once he had, Jack launched into his theory.

Chapter Seventy-Five
The Violin Rides Again

—

J ack placed the stratovarious gently on the ground in roughly the spot Vidalia had.

"So let me get this straight, make sure I understand the plan." Chase leaned back against the bench top that contained all the little cubbies from which Jack had gotten the strato. "Well, first there's the part ... um. Well, no. Oh yeah, that's right. We begin by ... Oh, no. Not that either. Oh, wait. That's right. You pretty much don't have a plan."

Jack sighed. "Well, I do. It just isn't fully formed yet."

"Oh, yeah. I remember." Chase crossed his arms unhappily. "First, we get the stratovarious down—check. Second, we make it grow up, which neither of us knows how to do. Right. Next, we fly it out of here. Again, neither of us knows how to do that, either. Whatever. Small stuff aside, next we fly to the Wargothe's house—in a place that, again, neither of us knows. Then we ring the doorbell, announce we're delivering a pizza, and walk in and get Pesky and Vidalia out—hopefully in one piece. Well, er, make that two, since there are two of them. Then we come home."

Jack agreed it sounded pretty hopeless but knew better than to tell Chase that. "Um. Yeah. In a nutshell, sure."

"Fine. I know we're not going to get past the second step in this, so since we're making a wish list, can I add my wish to the list? On the way back, can we stop off at The Golden Crust and get a pizza?"

"Whatever." Jack stared at the strato on the ground, wondering what would make it get bigger.

"Ok, but before we go for the gusto here, can I ask a stupid question?"

"Fine, but I'll count it as your third stupid question."

"If you failed so miserably at magic before, and if the strato needs magic to work, what makes you think you can get this thing off the ground? Or even get it to grow up?"

Jack examined the strato for a few seconds more before answering. "Call it *unfolding*, would you? Growing up sounds like this is a baby. Second, I did not fail miserably—"

Chase made hog-snorting noises under his breath.

"— Anyway, I don't think I would stand a chance on my own, but I'm hoping I won't have to. I'm hoping the Fyrelocke will do it for me." Jack smiled, and mockingly held the stone up for Chase to see.

Chase made a face, even less satisfied with that answer than he had been. "That thing? The only thing that rock has done is blow a giant hole in the floor of my room, and you think that's helpful?" He looked up. He always did while thinking. "I mean, I suppose it's helpful if I'm anti-floor, or if I happen to need a giant hole— which I didn't at the time. I was doing ok on the whole giant-hole thing— pretty caught up on all the giant holes I needed."

"That's not true. This thing helped me see that my parents were not themselves. It helped us to figure out that someone had been looking at the sheath of papers Trygg gave us, and it helped me to escape from the Cankrots—at least the first time."

"I'm not positive you didn't get out of that all on your own. You got out of the Wargothe's house without it."

"C'mon, Chase. Give me a break, will ya? Look, I'm positive they are at the Wargothe's house. I'm pretty sure I know what the Wargothe is planning. And if I'm right, we don't have a lot of time. Maybe I can't get this to work, but maybe I can. If I can but didn't— because I was too lazy to try—I'd be really mad at myself for it."

Jack went back to figuring out how to get the strato to unfold.

First, holding the Fyrelocke in one hand, he tried to wave his other hand at it in a flick similar to the way Vidalia flicked her wrist to cast a spell. Nothing happened. He tried waving his hands in the air, then his arms, then waving his arms in geometric shapes. Nothing seemed to work.

"Ok, calm down there, Frazzle. You look like you're trying to dance the Hokey Pokey. How about touching the Fyrelocke to it?"

Since nothing else was working, Jack figured why not.

The second he touched the Fyrelocke to the strato, it unfolded— growing in size, as if inflating.

Jack nodded at Chase, beaming. "Excellent."

The boys got inside.

"We're doing pretty well, so far." Jack smiled, taking the seat Vidalia had been in.

Chase looked uncomfortable. "Well, we're not dead yet. That's a plus. I thought for sure we'd be dead before we got to step two. So I figure we're probably ahead on this. So far, at least."

Jack ignored him and started looking around the compartment for controls, more out of habit than any real belief that it would have any. Stratovariouses have no controls. That was the problem with them.

Chapter Seventy-Six
We're Still Not Dead

––––

S o," Chase said conversationally after several minutes, "it's very
nice in here."

Jack ignored him again. He was not sure what to do next.
Vidalia had not done anything—no hand waving, no gestures, and no
golden sparks. How had she gotten the thing to move?

He tried touching the Fyrelocke to the dashboard. Nothing
happened.

Chase, undeterred, said, "Um. Yeah. Very nice in here. Much
more comfortable than our room. With our beds. Where we can
sleep. Yeah. That nice big room is nowhere near as good as this teeny
little ... er, thing."

Jack remembered that Vidalia had just kind of looked where she
wanted to go. So he tried it—staring at the little portal he knew was
in the corner of the workshop. He stared at it so long his eyes started
to water.

"Yeah. Sleeping in here might be tough. Unless you put your legs
up on that thing." Chase pointed at the dashboard. "And if I put my
legs down there, I suppose it would work. Hmm. You know, maybe
it would be easier to sleep in our room, now that I think about it.
Hey. Do you suppose maybe we could go back to our room? Now

there's an idea. Maybe make a frozen piz—whoa!"

Suddenly the stratovarious lifted off the ground.

"Hey, that's cool," Chase said, impressed. It did not last long though, as the stratovarious dipped in one corner and skidded loudly across the workshop floor.

"That can't be good."

Jack finally said something. "Yeah, I know. This isn't as easy as it looks."

"You're right. It looks so easy. I might have to try it myself. I think I'll watch the training video first, though. I hope the rental place has them. Think they have it in Blu-ray, surround sound?"

Jack got the stratovarious to begin moving toward the corner of the garage near the exit portal. "Relax, Chase. I know you're nervous, and that's why you're saying more junk even than you normally do—which is a lot anyway. Just relax, will you?"

"Me? Nervous? Hah!" He paused for a second as the strato knocked over a ladder that was propped against a wall in the workshop, and then said, "Uh. Hey, Jack?"

"What, Chase?" Impatience laced Jack's voice. He was having enough trouble trying to drive the thing than have to deal with Chase on top of everything.

"Well, there was that one part when Vidalia did that—"

They smashed into the wall, but the stratovarious bounced off. A small cascade of things that had been hanging on the wall of the workshop went crashing to the floor.

"… Yeah, that's what I mean," Chase said, "where she shrunk us down or something."

Chase was right. Jack stared at the portal trying to figure out how to do that. He tried touching the Fyrelocke to the dashboard again, which worked as well as it had the first time. So he gripped the Fyrelocke a little more tightly—hoping that might help—and imagined the strato shrinking in size.

For a while nothing happened. The stratovarious bobbed in the air while Jack tried to figure it out. Finally they started to shrink—everything around them seemed to balloon massively in size.

Chase nodded. "Wow. I honestly never thought you'd get this far. And we're still not dead." He patted Jack on the back.

"All right. Let's see if we can get this thing out of the workshop." There was some measure of confidence in Jack's voice.

That confidence evaporated quickly as they pummeled the portal aperture five or six times before Jack realized it did not open itself. After a few more sharpened jibes from Chase, Jack finally worked out the kinks of the portal, too.

They were out in the open night air.

The boys quickly realized what a difference it made flying at night. Earlier they could see for miles, limited only by hills in the distance or the ocean on the southern side. In the darkness, they could make out little except the few lights in the town below and a few of the brightest stars in the sky.

Without so much as a glow in the cabin and so little to go by outside, they were awash in a sea of inky blackness. Both boys grew disoriented— and more than a little closed in —it was hard to tell up from down.

"This thing have headlights?"

Based on what Vidalia had said, Jack was reasonably certain it did not. Besides, what good would headlights do when there was no road to light?

Chapter Seventy-Seven
On the Wing

H e was trying to find some clear marker on the ground—or where he thought the ground ought to be—to be sure the strato was oriented correctly when a loud clang echoed through their heads.

The strato jolted in the other direction.

Certain they had hit something, Jack realized that Chase was pointing in horror at a spike glinting brightly in the windscreen. It was affixed to an even larger spindle.

Unable to tell what it was, Jack asked, "What the heck is that?"

They felt the strato gently change direction and a periodic up-and-down movement.

Looking at the spike more closely, Jack realized it was a talon—larger than any he had ever seen in his life. Based on the size of that talon, the monster that held the strato must be gigantic.

"The Wargothe must have sent some monster to get us," he said. For once, Chase was speechless.

Before long, with what little light was coming in through the windshield, it became clear that the strato was being taken into a grove of trees. Branches whipped by at incredible speed.

Suddenly, the monster stopped on what appeared to be a tree

branch.

"Wait," Jack said. "That monster's not huge, we're just really small."

"Well, yeah, excellent deduction, Holmes."

"No. I mean, I don't think it's a monster."

Abruptly, the thing began clawing and clanging against the sides of the strato.

"That's great news." Chase had to yell to be heard over the banging. "So. All this noise is my imagination? Whew."

"I bet it's an owl," Jack yelled back.

"Oh, that's so much better. So he only wants to what? Eat us? I feel so relieved. Wow. And here I was concerned."

"I bet he's trying to break open the strato like a tortoise shell, but don't worry. Remember Vidalia said that this was made with the best in safety and protection charms. I don't think he can get in."

Chase did not relax. "Whew. See? Nothing to worry about. So why am I worried?"

If it was not for the sticky seats holding them in through all the jostling, the boys surely would have been tossed senseless against the inside walls of the stratovarious.

Before long, the bird—whatever it was—must have decided the strato was not very tasty and dropped it like a stone.

"Um, Jack." Hard to tell, but it seemed the ground was rapidly rising up to meet them. "Jack!" Chase said urgently.

Chapter Seventy-Eight
Your Destination Awaits

———

Jack saw very little that he could make out in near pitch-blackness, but the sensation of falling was unmistakable. He was struggling to ignore it and Chase's yelling, so he could concentrate on getting the strato moving again. Anywhere. It did not matter where as long as it was not directly into the ground.

The strato plummeted toward the forest floor. Blood flowed to Jack's head in panic—his face felt hot. Blinking furiously, the sting of sweat in his eyes, he felt himself tighten, bracing for impact. He tried to calm down and close his eyes—ignore the noise, the yelling and the sense of falling. He tried to picture the strato sailing up instead of into the soil.

Just as it seemed the strato was about to do exactly that, he wrested control at last. They sailed off at a slow clip through the trees. At least it seemed that they were going through the trees and not directly up or down. It was hard to tell for sure.

Superb. Plumb superb, young Jack.

With no flash of light or anything to announce the puriform's arrival, Trygg was suddenly seated on the third seat in the strato.

"Trygg," Jack said.

Chase turned to the seat next to him. "Bunny!"

And that, young Chase, is the reason I have withheld myself from you thus far. Shall I disappear right now? The puriform's face was deadpan, ears standing on end.

"Er, uh. No, Trygg—your honor."

Ah. "Your Honor." Now that's more like it.

"Trygg, you always come when it's too late. Couldn't you have come five minutes earlier?"

Chase nodded agreement but said nothing.

Again, you needed me not. Am I correct? It seems you did fine—as always—without my being there. Still, I will admit to correcting your course a bit. You seem to have an odd fondness for the ocean, which I assure you will do little good for either of us, but less for you.

Jack stared at the puriform. "When did you do that?"

Why, who do you suppose sent the owl? Or did you think owls often snack on midnight stratovariouses?

"You sent the owl?"

Well, yes, of course. Of course. The puriform paused and looked down at the floor of the strato. *Although I suppose I could simply have pushed you in a better direction, but what would be the fun in that? Besides, this killed two birds with one stone—as it were.*

Trygg gestured toward a white house, growing large in the windshield. During the discussion with the puriform neither of the boys had noticed it.

Voila! Your destination awaits.

Chapter Seventy-Nine
Wargothe Manor

T he boys stared in awe of the house, which had now grown so large in their eyes that it no longer fit in the windshield. Some of that, without a doubt, was because the strato itself was so small.

"Whoa," Chase said. "How could you not find that? It's beyond big."

"Trygg." Jack quickly scanned the interior of the strato in vain. "Ugh. Gone again." He turned back toward the house.

Chase gave a token glance, too, and then added, "I'm glad the bun … um, puriform came. I was kinda beginning to think you were making up this whole magic bunny thing for attention."

"Yeah, 'cause I would do that."

"Yeah—sad really," Chase said with no trace of sarcasm.

Jack turned back to the house. It was enormous—and completely, entirely and utterly white. It was lit up brightly in stark contrast to the backdrop of the nighttime sky behind it. From the angle at which they were approaching, the thing looked more like a fortress than a home. Beautifully decorated, gardens all around, a water fountain on the front lawn—it was more like a celebrity mansion in Hollywood than the home of a decaying, evil Wargothe.

Jack was trying to figure out how exactly to get in when he had an idea. Guiding the stratovarious all around the house, he was able to locate the window he had escaped from earlier in the day—still slightly ajar.

Gently, he maneuvered the strato in through the window and set it down beneath.

"You know, you really are starting to get the hang of this thing," Chase said with a nod.

"Open. Release," Jack said, freeing himself of the stratovarious' safety restraint system—he unstuck himself. Chase did the same, and the boys climbed through the door on the side as the strato finished growing to its full size.

They drifted silently through the cellar, trying doors as they went. Chase tried the first, a room that amounted to nothing more than a broom closet, before Jack had a chance to warn him of the shocking he could get. After that, Chase left the door-checking to Jack and his wallet.

They found the room where Jack had been earlier, now empty, the door replaced on its hinges.

"Whoa, this room is creepy. You think the strange kid stayed here?" Chase asked in a hushed whisper.

"Yeah. Newt," Jack said, looking around the room again.

"Well, someone stayed here for a long time." Chase stared in mild disgust and pointed at the bed. "Either that or you left one heckuva stain for such a short stay."

"Cut it out, Chase."

Jack had been hoping they would find Pesky and Vidalia here, and that maybe there would be a quick way to free them and leave. He had hoped that giving Vidalia the Fyrelocke was all he had to do. From there, the Warlocke would do the rest.

He had not wanted a direct run-in with the Wargothe.

Now it seemed more likely that they would have to go through the Wargothe to find Pesky and Vidalia.

The next room they checked was filled, floor to ceiling on every wall, with little cubbies similar to the one Vidalia had taken the strato from in the Dorfnutters' workshop. The cubbies all contained the same thing—each had a fyrestone. The room had hundreds and hundreds of fyrestones in different shapes, sizes and colors.

"How do you know they aren't empty geodes?"

"I can tell." That was all Jack would say.

After searching uneventfully through the cellar, the boys made their way upstairs. They cringed at each squeak of the stairwell.

Chapter Eighty
From the Fyre to the Flames

On the main floor, everything was eerily quiet. They crept along the hallway, peeking into doorways and finding nothing.

The opulence of the upper floor was as stunning as the outside of the manor had been. Although Jack had been here before, his head had been clouded with the sleep spell that was cast before being brought to the Wargothe. He could not remember much of what he now saw.

He did remember the way Oleagina Cankrot had taken him from the main chamber—where he had met the Wargothe—to the stairs leading to the cellar. He tried his best to reverse that track, thinking it possible that the Wargothe would be in the same dimly lit hall.

They came to a large set of double doors and stood somber outside them. After a moment, Chase asked in a low voice, "How's that plan coming?"

"I've got nothing." Jack looked around furtively. "I'm going to take a look in there. If he's there, I want you to stay back and see if you can track down Vidalia or Pesky. I'll do what I can."

Chase moved to the side, and Jack opened the door a crack to peek into the room. But the doors themselves wrested control from him and opened fully.

As it became clear the room was indeed occupied, he did a little jig trying to decide whether to hide or be bold. Finally, doors flung wide, his indecision left him only the option of boldness.

The dark-robed form of the Wargothe stood in the middle of the room, leaning over a table. The chamber was extremely bright, but from where he stood, Jack could not make out what was on the table.

"Ah. Boomershine. I must admit to a bit of surprise at your arrival tonight—and not late for the party." The robed figure did not bother to turn around.

Jack knew it made no difference what he did now, so he stepped into the room a few paces.

The doors behind him closed with a distinct and final-sounding click.

Don't worry, Jack. I've got your back. A voice rang through his head, though a little fuzzy.

"Trygg?" Jack whispered, but the voice did not have the same quality as the puriform's.

No, and if I were you, I wouldn't answer out loud. He can hear you. The voice was clearer now. Jack knew the "he" meant the Wargothe.

Just think your answers loudly. I'll hear them well enough. But no, Trygg— while far more powerful at magic than I could ever be—cannot come to this place. You know that. Those pure of thought—and Trygg is a puriform—cannot fight pure evil. But I can. My family invented evil, after all.

"You've arrived in time to watch the fireworks." The robed figure troubled himself to lift his head this time so that he seemed to be calling up toward the ceiling. He finished by sniffing the air strangely.

For a second, Jack thought the voice in his head might be the Wargothe's own but then realized it could not be. He wondered if the Wargothe could hear the voice, too, somehow.

No, he can't hear me—only you. Relax. He can't see in your mind anymore.

Earlier, you didn't have me to stop him from it, but now you do. He's confused by it, but he will never tell you that.

Who are you? Jack thought as loudly as he could.

You know who I am. The Fyrelocke buzzed slightly from where Jack had it tucked away. *And stop shouting, will you?*

Ignatius. The realization struck Jack, suddenly.

Very good.

Jack took a closer look at the table and realized with horror that Vidalia's curly blonde hair was sticking out from behind the Wargothe.

An eye to the side of the table confirmed Jack's suspicions—there stood a shiny metal stand with a cup-shaped holder. On the stand was a small fist-sized geode. Although he knew the geode to be an empty one, he had no idea how he knew.

This was bad. How could he possibly get Vidalia out of this?

Jack. This was what you had to do all along. You have everything you need now to free the Warlocke, to save Vidalia. More than you need. It does not matter now who the Warlocke is. All that matters is that you make him think you are. I'll try to provide the rest—like I helped you drive a stratovarious to get here. You can do this.

Jack realized Ignatius was right. He knew what the Wargothe was planning to do, and he also knew exactly what sour result there would be if the Wargothe chose wrong. He had read too many case histories—provided by Trygg—not to know with certainty what the result would be. Jack would never be the same—schizophrenia, dementia. But the Wargothe would never be the same, either. He would be shattered and useless.

Doubt.

That was Jack's best weapon now. As he thought about it, he realized that Ignatius had given him the last key he needed. He easily had enough now to cast plenty of doubt in the Wargothe's mind.

R. Christopher Kobb

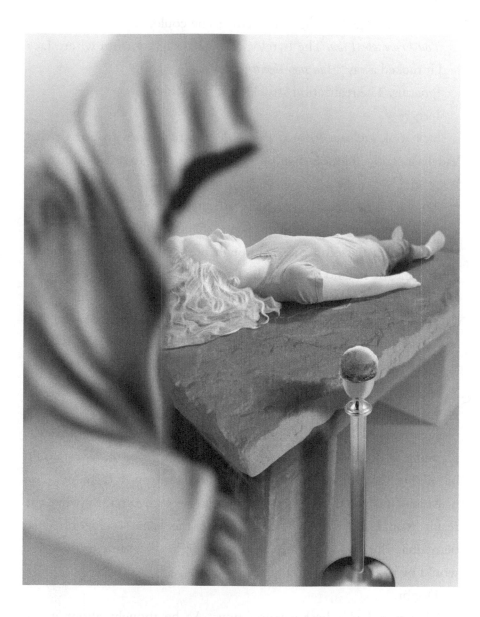

212

Chapter Eighty-One
The Crux of It All

T he Wargothe had not turned—had only finished sniffing the air when Jack said to his back, "Hah!" He had not meant to do that, exactly. He knew he had to instill doubt in the Wargothe and was trying to decide how to begin, when the word spilled from his mouth.

The Wargothe spun around, pure hatred painted across his withered face. "You think this is a game, boy?"

"Um, I meant ..." He struggled to think what to say. He knew he had to make his move and decided to come right out with it. "She's not the Warlocke," he said.

Despite his ire, the Wargothe's face had hardly any color. It was gray and sunken, shriveled and peppered with cracks and crevices—wrinkles within wrinkles. Being eye-to-eye with the ancient and "mighty" Wargothe left Jack with a slight tremble. Did the battered old man notice?

"I mean ..." He decided to take a chance. "I am the first person ever to get out of your grasp, and I did it not once but twice. I am the first person ever to escape your manor, and I am the first to ever break back in. She lies there helpless, easily captured, and you think she is the Warlocke?"

He knew the words were hardly fair to Vidalia, but he could not worry about that now. He caught the wince, knowing he had struck home the second he saw it flit quickly across the Wargothe's face.

Jack had known it from that moment standing in the Dorfnutters' spare room, but looking at his face, he knew it with all certainty. The Wargothe was the man in the picture he had seen—the woodcut at the bottom of the stack of papers the boys had sorted through. It had been labeled "Aaron James Cross."

"The Warlocke would be hard to capture—harder to keep." He quoted lyrically, "The Warlocke appears / Locke's Fyre bearing." He dramatically plucked the Fyrelocke from his pocket and held it high. "I am the Warlocke, not her."

Spittle clung from the Wargothe's lip as he looked on Jack with interest, gawking at the rock in his hand. "Why, may I ask, would that matter in the least?" He stood shaking, trying to contain an endless, seething rage—but uncertainty had crept into his voice.

"Blood," Jack said quietly. "Locke blood, specifically." He took three measured paces closer. The two were now only about ten apart. "You are a thousand years old."

The ancient man allowed enough time for a small pause and then said with a smirk, "For a man of a thousand years, I have held together pretty well. Pretty well, indeed." At that inopportune moment, the Wargothe's arm fell off with a dull thud as it thwacked the ground.

"Blast it all and back." He stooped to retrieve the arm. Once he had, he again wedged it into the socket accompanied by a disgusting, wet, crunching sound. After he was done, he added as an afterthought, "All things considered."

He took a step closer to Jack. "Ok, then. So you think I am some forty generations old? That's not possible, and you know it."

"No. Not only is it possible, it is true. And the father of all modern magic would have no problem doing it."

"So you think I'm Aaron James Cross?" the Wargothe asked.

"Of course not. He was killed almost a thousand years ago by none other than Ephraim Locke." Jack looked him in the eye. "You."

Jack went on. "You took his place, pretended to be him. As Ephraim, you had made a reputation for yourself—it was not a good one. Aaron James had a great reputation. People loved him. So in the moment, you quickly darkened your hair and changed your name."

"Absolutely contrary to all the recorded histories, but if you were right—and I am not saying you are—I ask again: Why would that matter in the least?" The Wargothe had a malicious, challenging gleam in his eye.

"It matters because of all your experimentation. All your practice sessions left little but a wake of comatose and schizophrenic victims, until you finally realized that it worked only when you used family members. Relatives. Blood relatives."

"Used them for what?" He said the word with a sharp, impatient snap.

"What else could you possibly want? For the man who has everything, what is left?" Jack felt sick doing it, but he had to play the game. He had to make Ephraim feel it. He smiled broadly as he said, "But you do seem to need a new body."

He stood as still as he could and looked directly into the Wargothe's eyes. "Hundreds of fyrestones, and as many coma-related deaths or schizophrenic patients, before you finally worked out the main problem you'd been having. Blood relatives. Transferring to a new body would work only if both people were related. And I tell you now that I—not Vidalia—am a Locke. It's my body you want. Not hers."

Jack relaxed his shoulders and stood at ease. "I am the Warlocke."

Something snapped in the Wargothe's face.

Chapter Eighty-Two
Confrontation

——

Literally, something snapped in the Wargothe's face, which abruptly sagged and then hung slack. It held no emotion, but his body language said all that needed saying. Besides, Jack had heard him curse "Blast it all" enough to know what he was trying to get out. Perhaps it was something with a little extra, like "Blast it all to little bits and pieces" or "Blast it into outer space." Certainly one of those or something inconceivably more creative than Jack could ever imagine.

The furious Wargothe waved his arm about—the one that had not yet fallen off—and green sparks showered over his face, reanimating it with a detail Jack had not yet seen. Ephraim Locke threw a small temper tantrum—kicking and screaming, punching and wailing.

"Blast it. Blast it. Blast it!" He ran in a circle, kicking things. Jack was reasonably sure the Wargothe had done some kind of permanent damage to one of his feet from kicking the base of the stone slab table. The sound did not seem a happy one.

"How did a stupid twelve-year-old brat of a kid figure out in a day what I needed centuries to discover? How? How? I ask you."

Wild-eyed and seething, the thing that stood nose to nose with Jack was inhuman. Again, this was one of those questions best left unanswered, and Jack did just that.

The elder man squinted. His eyes went keen as he appraised the boy. "Ah. Perhaps, though, I can say you are a brat of a kid, but stupid you are not."

The Wargothe stood woodenly for a moment and then smiled as fully as his dried lips would allow, a sudden shift in his temperament. "My, my, my. Boomershine is a clever boy. Perhaps more than clever, after all. Perhaps, but are you a Locke?" The Wargothe stood rubbing his chin thoughtfully—carefully—Jack had seen what happened when he was not careful.

He stood silently by, waiting.

"This is an important question," the Wargothe said. "I only have one shot at this, and if I am wrong, I will spend the rest of my days in a new body—yours, as it were—but in torment and a body of little other use. On the other hand," it seemed a calculated afterthought, "so would you. Or maybe just part of you." He said it with a careful fascination at Jack's response.

Jack gave none.

"Young Boomershine, if I was to believe you and you are the Warlocke, why would you come offering yourself up to me?" He smiled his reptilian smile. "Hmm?"

"Um." Why had he not seen that coming?

The truth was that Vidalia was the Warlocke, and he needed her to be safe, so she could eventually defeat the Wargothe herself. Obviously, that answer would not work.

"Um."

Ignatius, somewhere in the Fyrelocke, was offering nothing in the way of help. Jack shot a glance at Vidalia's curly hair tucked behind her head as she lay unconscious on the table behind Ephraim. He struggled to come up with something.

With that darting look, the Wargothe misconstrued and smiled.

"Ahhhhh. Now I understand."

"What? Wait. No … It's not that. Um. I, um …"

With each punctuated, stuttered denial by Jack, the Wargothe visibly became more convinced that he had guessed correctly.

"How terribly chivalrous of you, young Boomershine. A knight in shining armor, come to save your hapless damsel in distress. Well, you need not have worried. You think I would leave such an important decision to chance? I have a spell at my ready that can tell me what I need to know. It requires the smallest sample of blood." At that, he jabbed his hand toward Jack, who registered a sharp pain across his palm before he realized green sparks were drifting lazily down from the air between them. His hand was left with a small bleeding gash that stung more than it should have for its size.

Don't worry. I'll handle this. Ignatius' voice returned as a whisper inside Jack's head.

"There we go," Ephraim said, looking at a small vial with the tiniest amount of blood in it. "If you are the Warlocke and she is not, then I will gladly let her go. And you shall have her spot."

Why did it sting so much for a drop of blood?

Dark Magic. It's like that, Ignatius explained. *The magic itself takes pleasure from causing pain. Or rather, it might be more accurate to say that pain and misery fuel the spells further. That's what makes dark magic so effective. So dangerous. That's what makes those who would wield it so horribly corrupt.*

Whatever Ephraim had done, thick green smoke was now pouring from the vial.

"Excellent," he said. "Ah, young Boomershine, you did not lie after all. You are undoubtedly a Locke." He held up the vial, which was petering out small remnants of vapor. "Why, I have your pedigree right here."

Ignatius had done it somehow.

"Congratulations." The Wargothe smiled.

Chapter Eighty-Three
Conflagration

C ongratulations, indeed.

The moment the words left the Wargothe's lips, Vidalia disappeared—transpositioned someplace else—and he beckoned Jack over.

"True, I could easily place you there myself, but you pledged your cooperation, and now I shall put your promise to the test. Young Boomershine, if you would be so kind to remove your shirt and lie upon the table."

Jack took a few steps closer, looked questioningly at the table and walked past the shiny metal stand holding the empty geode.

Ephraim apparently caught Jack's eye and reassured him. "Don't worry. I have kept my side of the bargain. She has been released and is now safe."

Jack was certain he had done no such thing, but it did not matter now. He had accomplished what needed to be done. Now the Wargothe would be managed. He would attempt the soul transplant but would quickly discover that Jack was not a Locke. By then, it would be too late.

More than saving Vidalia, Jack stood a real chance of undoing the Wargothe himself. It had to be done.

Vidalia was ok. She would be freed somehow once the Wargothe's power was gone. He hoped Chase was looking for Pesky, or maybe the two of them were now looking for Vidalia together. With any luck, they would find her, and they could all get out ok.

Jack's fate was not so easily remedied.

Before Jack got too close to the table, the Wargothe insisted on collecting the Fyrelocke. Jack had known that was coming and gave up the fyrestone willingly—almost cheerfully.

The Wargothe eyed the rock with fascination. "Ah. Perspective changes everything, does it not, Boomershine? A thousand years of knowledge I have gained and experiences I have had since I have last seen this." He held it higher and aimed a goading smile at Jack. "Finally, it has become little more than another to add to my collection. Not so powerful as I once remembered. I feel the power in it, and, in fact, I have others that have more power than this one, easily," he said proudly.

The stone slab was cold on Jack's bare back. Other than the fact that the Wargothe had probably always done it this way—had people remove their shirts—Jack saw no reason for it.

Glowing green bands of light held him to the table.

That was not necessary. At this point, he had done all that he could. There was nothing left to do but follow orders. To fight now would only jeopardize Vidalia—the Warlocke. He could not let that happen. He would not.

He gave one last thought to his parents, hoping they would be ok, before his mind turned to the distant memory Ignatius had shown him. Ignatius' soul had been ripped, screaming, from his body and sucked into a fyrestone on a stand. Jack would experience the same firsthand.

He tried not to imagine how badly it was going to hurt.

Chapter Eighty-Four
Window of Hopelessness

W here are we?"

Chase spun around from the wall screen he had been watching. "Vid ... Vidalia." He ran over to help her up. "Are you ok?"

"Yeah. I'm fine. Just a bit ... I don't know ... out of sorts, I guess. Where are we?" she asked again.

"Um." He looked around. "It's the room where they kept Jack earlier. He thinks it's the same one they kept Newt in."

"Who?"

"I'll explain later. Come on. Watch what's happening, and I'll try to explain what I know."

He explained how—not long after Jack went through the large double-doors—Chase suddenly popped in to the holding room. Not in the least certain how he had gotten there, he speculated that maybe the Wargothe knew he was in the hall and captured him. Or maybe it was another member of the Society of All Magicks, but Chase had seen no one. Barely taking breaths, he explained that immediately upon his arrival the wall had filled with a view of what was going on where Jack and the Wargothe were. Not like a television, it was a three-dimensional view into the room where Jack lay, almost a window without glass. It changed perspective as they moved. Chase explained that—although it looked fully three-dimensional—it was nothing more than a vision in the wall. He had tried to help Jack but bounced right off.

"My shoulder still stings," he said, moving it around. "Anyway, this wasn't here when we snuck in and found the room earlier."

"Why do you think it's here now?" Vidalia did not look at Chase. She was transfixed with what was going on in the wall screen.

"I think the Wargothe is showing off. I think he wanted me—and now you—to see him win."

"That's the Wargothe?" she asked.

"Yes. Ephraim Locke."

"That's Ephraim Locke?" She softened her voice and said, "No way. It can't be. He died centuries ago."

Chase explained everything he had seen in the vision-screen, including Jack's encounter with the Wargothe and the transpositioning of Vidalia to the room—though he had not known it when she had disappeared from view in the wall screen image.

"Hey, where's Pesk … er, your dad?"

Vidalia considered for a moment. "I don't know. I hope he's all right. I remember us looking for Jack, but that's the last thing I can recall. My head feels pretty hazy. I hope he's ok."

Chase tried to reassure her with speculation that maybe they were keeping her father in a different room with higher security. After all, Jack had escaped from this room a few hours before.

Vidalia attempted a few spells to see if there was some way out, but the walls shot back. Luckily, the fiery green detonations missed them both, but they impressively charred the floor wherever they hit. She gave up in case the next one did not miss them.

Something was happening in that other room. They both turned to watch the screen.

Chapter Eighty-Five
A Wargothe's Puzzle

———

T here you go, young Boomershine," the Wargothe said with his wasted, throaty voice. "Slip into it nice and easy— picture it, feel it. It will be easier that way. I can pluck you, if you force me, but this will be much, much easier." His voice trailed off in a hiss.

Ephraim could not believe it was finally about to end. He had waited centuries for this moment.

As the boy had proclaimed, it had taken him centuries to realize that it might be possible, and centuries more before he discovered most of the pieces. Add another hundred years before he discovered the final crucial piece. As a puzzle that gets more difficult the longer you stare at it, so was this. As with that puzzle, the moment you realize what you had gotten wrong, it all seems so simple.

How could it ever have taken so long?

With every passing year along the way, he had to discover more patching spells that might fix this problem or that malfunction with his aging, decaying, frail body.

Chapter Eighty-Six
Green Lightning

J ack was breathing heavily as he lay on the stone bench. It was
cold and hard on his back. He felt a tingling across his skin, and
then a glow flitted over him like green lightning. Humming and
crackling static filled the air.

He glanced nervously over at the fyrestone perched on the shiny
brass holder.

Chapter Eighty-Seven
The Jack of Spades

———

The humming grew louder, the green glow more intense.

Ephraim, the Wargothe, gave the boy one final push—a sudden flash of green light formed up around Jack's body, sizzled and raced to the stone at the top of the brass geode stand. A sharp crack echoed throughout the room. The smell of ozone filled the air, and it was over. The newly made fyrestone on the stand lit brightly as a green ember for a moment then dimmed completely. The stand teetered unsteadily for a moment while the geode sizzled and hissed. Green smoke poured down from it.

Jack's body went limp.

Ephraim cackled and leapt at the stand, swiped the stone up, and held it high in the air. He felt Boomershine's power surge from within it. A furtive squint at the body, a quick mind-probe to confirm that the boy was now only a shell—soulless and empty—and the Wargothe jumped in the air with glee.

"I have done it."

He danced around the room with no grace to speak of. The hard part was over. He never thought he would be able to get the Warlocke to surrender and provide his own body and soul for the transfer so easily. If he had to force Jack from his body, even a bit, there could have been undesirable results, perhaps permanent damage. A number of the experiments he had done that way had not gone well. Although they had worked, there could be complications—most of them minor but bothersome. He could not believe his luck in executing this so perfectly—not a scratch on the boy and absolutely no internal damage—the soul transfer would be a stunning success.

"I've done it. I've done it." He chanted the words as he sauntered clumsily about the room. "I have the Warlocke's soul in my palm."

He drew the rock down to study and sniffed it. "Poor Boomershine, I must say you weren't nearly so powerful as I would have thought, but that's ok," he consoled the rock, "I shall remedy that presently."

He set the fyrestone gently into the brass holder and pulled himself onto the twin of the stone slab on which Jack's body lay.

Chapter Eighty-Eight
One Fyrestone, One Soul

Vidalia was sobbing inconsolably on Chase's shoulder.

He stood with fury, watching, out of the corner of his eye, the Wargothe dance around foolishly. Heat and anger burned his face.

Now he understood why Jack was sick to his stomach after seeing Ignatius go through this. Now he understood what was in that dumb rock. Not a repository of magic, but a soul. A person.

His friend.

He could not speak. Besides, what could he say to Vidalia? What was there to say?

Chapter Eighty-Nine
A Soul-Change Operation

———

Shirtless, Ephraim hummed to himself distractedly as he got ready for the second half of the operation. After such a long time focused on finding the solution to his problem, with single-minded concentration and little else to interest him, now that he was so close to resolution, he actually felt a little sad.

For centuries this had been his only pursuit, and now it was about to end. And because he knew the patching, repair and maintenance spells so well, and he knew to begin employing them long before middle age—when he had begun the spells on his own body— Boomershine's body would likely last three times as long.

Despite his small bit of regret, he lay down excitedly on the stone slab askance from Jack's bench. He could barely contain himself.

His arm fell off to the side of the table, and he let it lie, closing his eyes in concentration.

Before long, the same electric green glow ebbed and flowed over his worn body. It crackled and hissed. Smoke rose, and the mighty Wargothe began to twitch.

Energy coalesced around the Wargothe, and in a final shot, it rocketed out at Jack's lifeless body. It flowed all around him, surged through him, made a loud crack in the air, and disappeared in a swirl in his abdomen. Silence reigned, but the room was cloudy with green, hazy smoke.

No sooner had the green glow disappeared from Jack's body than a loud poof and a cloud of foul, green smoke erupted from the Wargothe's. Exhausted beyond all possibility of holding together even a second longer—and without Ephraim's soul to bind it—it collapsed into dust.

Chapter Ninety
Ghastly Anticipation

———

T he Wargothe's body was gone, but Chase knew where his soul went. He had seen the surge of power flow directly into Jack's motionless body—the powerful green lightning pitched in a swirling tide directly into him. He knew it with all certainty: The operation had worked.

Vidalia was still sobbing but had calmed somewhat. They watched in rapt attention to see what would happen in that other room. Chase had caught her up on as much as he could, having explained that they knew her to be the Warlocke—although she did not believe him. He had done his best to explain why Jack pretended to be the Warlocke, though he did not completely understand himself, but he thought he had gotten most of it out correctly.

He had explained what he had come to understand only while watching the action in the wall, before Vidalia had been transpositioned into the room with him. If the Wargothe had tried to do this before Jack's soul was moved from his body into a geode, they would both be trapped forever and would appear schizophrenic. After Jack's soul had moved, if his body was not a blood relative, then the Wargothe would have been trapped and would experience severe debilitating dementia. Either way, the outcome was not a good one for the Wargothe, but either way, it was worse for Jack.

No matter what, though, Jack was no more. Ephraim Locke—in whatever form he ended up in: schizophrenic, demented or stronger than ever—now controlled that body. Chase did not want to know which it was. He could not be happy with any of those ends. They watched, consumed by dread, as Jack's body lay limp for several minutes, off in that other room. Neither could speak, or move, or even blink.

Chapter Ninety-One

It's Alive

———

The Wargothe's ashes smoldered under the charred remains of the brown robe. Wafting puffs of smoke released periodically into the air. Chase realized he was holding his breath and had to force himself to breathe.

The thing that was inside Jack twitched.

It twitched again.

Chase and Vidalia stood horrified. Chase was torn between wanting to see Jack move yet knowing that it would not be the Jack he knew doing the moving, and so he found himself hoping the thing did not move at all. But it did.

Suddenly its eyes opened.

The thing-that-looked-like-Jack rubbed its eyes groggily and sat up from the table. It looked around once and gazed down incredulously at Jack's body—beaming from ear to ear and touching its head, each arm and leg, and its chest to be sure everything was all there. It hopped down spritely from the bench.

Chase could not believe his eyes. The operation had worked exactly as the Wargothe had planned.

A little unsteady on its feet but moving without a hitch, the thing put on Jack's shirt and left the room.

Chapter Ninety-Two
It's Here

Trapped in the holding room, Chase and Vidalia were in a panic.

Remembering how Jack had gotten out earlier, Chase had tried the hinges long before Vidalia had arrived. They were well protected now.

They were trying to think of ways to get out, when the almost-imperceptible protective spell around the room stopped and the wall-screen disappeared. With the spell gone, the quiet hum that had filled the room was gone. Chase had not noticed it before, but in its absence, he knew it had been there the entire time. The room was truly silent now, and the two stared at the door suspiciously.

The doorknob jiggled. It turned. The door opened wide, and the thing-that-looked-like-Jack stood blinking at them with a funny smile across its face, eyes glazed.

Chapter Ninety-Three
Bonds, Municipal and Other

———

Chase watched as Vidalia did something with her hands, and a bolt of green light shot out and smacked the thing-that-looked-like-Jack right in the face. There was an instant where an expression of shock crossed its face, and one panicked "wait" escaped before it was slammed backward into the wall behind the open doorway.

The thing was piled in a heap against the stone wall, leaving the doorway free.

"Whoa, that was wicked." Chase grinned. "Let's go."

"Wait. Something's not right." She walked over to the boy slumped against the wall and looked him over.

"What?" Chase was confused. They needed to get out before the Wargothe—in his new body—came to.

"I ... uh ... I don't know, but I'm not sure that's the Wargothe." She bit her lip.

It had to be the Wargothe, Chase was certain. They had seen the soul-transplant operation work flawlessly.

"It doesn't make any sense. That spell should not have hurt the Wargothe much. That spell should not have hurt the Wargothe at all. I thought it might buy us a few seconds."

Chase was suddenly all ears. "You mean, you think that's Jack?"

"I don't know. I don't see how, but the Wargothe should not have … well, I would have thought he could easily deflect that spell. It's only a second-level dark magic spell. Maybe it's a trap."

"A trap? We were already gift-wrapped in a locked room. How much more trapped could he need us to be?" Chase paused for a second and then realized something. "Wait, did you say that was dark magic? Is that why it was green?"

Staring at Jack's unconscious body, Vidalia shrugged and said, "Yes. Why?"

"Well, isn't it banned or something? Like, you could get strung up by your fingernails for using it or something? How do you know how to use dark magic, anyway?" He eyed her suspiciously.

She giggled in response. "Yes, it's banned but not for self-defense. Everyone learns some but only enough for protection." She pointed at Jack lying on the floor. "Should we do something, you think?"

"Um."

Chase was sure they were both thinking the same thing: If it was the Wargothe, they would be making a big mistake to hang around—they were not likely to get a second chance. If it was Jack, they would be making a big mistake to leave him.

Vidalia spoke up. "Well, I suppose we could wait till he wakes up and see what we think then. The first sign that it isn't Jack, we run and try to get back to the strato you came in. We already bought more time than I was hoping for."

That sounded as good as anything Chase could come up with. Unless it was financial planning, all other planning was Jack's area—not Chase's. At the moment, Jack was in no position to help, and nobody needed any advice on municipal bonds.

Chapter Ninety-Four
The Life Cycle of a Wargothe

T he thing-that-looked-like-Jack, which probably was not Jack but might be, moved and let out a groan.

In the off chance that it was him, they had moved him away from the wall and tried to prop up his head a little with a roll of paper towels they had found in the broom closet.

Chase was worried for him yet secretly hoping he would perform some gross bodily function as he was coming to. *That would be perfect.* He realized how childish he was being and put on a serious face. He was more worried about Jack, anyway.

Vidalia paced anxiously back and forth.

The thing let out another groan and shifted its legs around.

Abruptly its eyes opened.

"Don't move. Who are you?" Vidalia yelled down at it.

The thing closed its eyes and groaned. "I'll be whoever you want me to be, if you'll make the sledge hammer go away."

"Seriously. Who are you?"

"Ok. Ok. I'm Jack. Now will you make the funny little lightning bugs go away, too?"

Vidalia looked at Chase. "Quick. Think of a question to ask him."

He looked wide-eyed at her for a second, then said, "Uh ... Um

… how many innings in a baseball game?"

Vidalia kicked him. "I mean a question only Jack can answer."

"Oh. Um, uh … Who beat you up and stole your lunch money when you were in the second grade?"

"Chase." Jack growled. "Really?"

"Better tell us, or we won't believe you're Jack," he said in a singsong chant.

Jack moaned his impatience, but then yielded. "Elvis Pretzel."

Vidalia said, "Well, he's clearly not Jack, or his brain has been—"

"It's him," Chase told her.

"What? 'Elvis Pretzel?'"

"His real name is Alvin Pittso. We just call him that." Chase smiled.

Jack had his eyes closed, rubbing his temples, as he added, "And he didn't beat me up. I've told you a hundred times, I tripped."

Chase smiled. "Yeah, right." He turned to Vidalia and said, "When we found them, Elvis was standing above Jack, who was lying on the ground." He glanced quickly at the boy on the ground. "He seems to do that a lot. Anyway, I'm sure he's right. He—only—tripped." He emphasized each word, dramatically bobbing his head, eyes wide.

"Look. I've got one heckuva headache here. Why don't you guys go ahead. I'll catch a quick nap and be right behind you."

Vidalia giggled, flaring golden light over him. His eyes opened wide, and he sprang to life, hopping up from the ground.

"Wow. I feel great."

"A little healing spell," she said with a wink, "but the energy is a side effect—don't get too used to it. It wears off."

"Wow." Chase agreed as he appraised Jack and turned to Vidalia. "Can you do that to me, too?"

"Sure, but I'd have to hit you with the Slam spell first." She stood back and raised her hands.

Chase wasted no time putting up his hands and begging out. "Um. You know, um, suddenly, I think I've changed my mind."

"Suit yourself." Vidalia shrugged and turned back to Jack. "So what happened?"

"Yeah," Chase said, "We saw you on the wall-screen. It looked like you got zapped."

Jack had no idea they were able to see what had been going on, so after asking Chase to explain the wall-screen, he launched into what had happened after he had gotten into the room with the Wargothe.

"Well first, right after I walked in, Ignatius started talking to me. He told me I could do what needed to be done, and he'd help where he could."

Jack had to explain that part to Vidalia. She had never known what lay at the center of the Fyrelocke—Ignatius.

"He kept talking to you after you gave up the Fyrelocke?" she asked with surprise. She explained that most of what she knew about fyrestones was from lore, but all that lore left it reasonably clear that fyrestones worked only while you held them.

"No, I never gave up the Fyrelocke."

"But we saw you," Chase said.

"No, you saw me give up one of the fyrestones I swiped from the stone room. When you weren't looking, I took two of them."

"It fooled Ephraim Locke?" Vidalia was incredulous.

"He hadn't seen or held it in a thousand years."

"Yeah," Chase added as an aside to Vidalia, "there's like a million of them in that room. There's no way I'd be able to tell them apart. What made you think to take some?"

Jack thought for a moment. "I don't know. Maybe Ignatius knew I'd need them, and prodded me to take them? I don't know. Anyway," Jack went on, "so I gave him one of the fyrestones when he asked for the Fyrelocke, but I had swiped two. So the other I switched with the empty that was sitting on the stand next to the slab table."

"You did not—we watched the whole thing. We never saw you do that."

Chase chuckled. "He's wicked good at sleight of hand."

After a quick explanation—and a demonstration to appease Vidalia's curiosity—she said, "Wow. That would be the only way to fool the Wargothe. If you had used magic, he would have sensed it right away. He didn't notice that the geode was now … er, uh … occupied?"

"I guess not, but why would he? He knew it was empty before. Why would he check it again? As far as I know, he didn't check it again until after he thought my soul went into it. About that, I'm not sure what happened. To be honest, I'm not sure if my soul couldn't go in the geode because it was … uh, full, or if Ignatius did something. All I know is after that, Ignatius somehow helped me relax and blocked Ephraim from seeing into me. So it looked like my body was empty to him."

Both Chase and Vidalia were so focused on Jack, they did not blink.

"At that point, if Ignatius had done no more, when the Wargothe transferred his soul to me, we would both have been trapped together forever. Luckily, he did one more thing. He deflected the Wargothe's soul. Well, maybe deflected is the wrong word. It was more like he redirected it."

"Redirected it where?" they asked at the same time.

"In here." He held up a fyrestone, a slightly different color and shape than the Fyrelocke. "The empty one I'd taken from the stand when I switched it for the full one."

A throat cleared. A deep, booming voice said, "I'll take that."

Chapter Ninety-Five
A Fyregothe

T he voice belonged to none other than Pescipalius Dorfnutter himself. He belly laughed at their reactions and smiled around, finishing with Jack. "Very good. Bah! I say excellent, m'boy. You've done incredibly well. I never thought I would see the day when the Wargothe would succumb to the tricks of a twelve-year-old boy, and all without the use of magic." He was so excited he was practically yelling.

Vidalia bristled. "Well, that's hardly true. Ignatius used magic for him."

Pesky smiled affectionately at his daughter. "Well, true, true, my dear, but Vee, I think you may be forgetting the importance of this. Ignatius could no more defeat the Wargothe by himself than an ice lolly could. On the other hand, Boomershine here has persevered several times against the last-remaining, first-rate wizard—and one with over a thousand years of experience in both magics besides. All the while, Jack without direct access to any magic whatever." He beamed at the boy.

"Splendid. Good job, I say." Pesky slapped Jack hard on the back, while Vidalia turned dour. "Please do allow me to lighten you of that burden." He plucked the newly made fyrestone from Jack's raised hand. "I realize it may not appear so, but this is actually quite a dangerous little item you have—this, ah, *Fyregothe*, as it were. Perhaps more powerful, and I don't mean that in a good way, than the Fyrelocke itself. I must ensure it stays out of the hands of those who would do harm using it."

"Ah, but here is an interesting bit." With that, he held up the fyrestone for them all to see. The outer shell shimmered and disappeared. Inside, as when Vidalia had shown them the crystalline center of the Fyrelocke, were glistening shards of the mineral gem at its center. By contrast, the shards in the Fyregothe had a deep forest-green color that lightened toward the tip at each crystalline point.

"Emerald, it is. I have never heard of a fyrestone with an emerald core," Pesky said with a trace of admiration. He allowed the view inside for another brief moment before he stuffed the stone into a pocket somewhere in his vest and clapped his hands. "Now. You three had best jot out of here. This is a safe house for the Society of All Magicks, and I don't doubt that some of their number will arrive shortly. I intend to do my best to detain them until some authorities have had a chance to arrive."

He turned to Vidalia. "Vee, you get these boys back to the house and, as you do, put a trace on your strato. When you get back, have Bea contact Mr. Dodder and Mr. Wimple to gather the authorities and follow the trail. I will most assuredly need some assistance before too long. So make it quick, and I shall see you back home as soon as I am able." He kissed the top of her head.

"Again, a great job to all of you. You were most amazing and most effective in this." He smiled as big a smile as Jack had ever seen him wear and gave a glowing wink to Vidalia in particular as he emphasized the words and said, "All of you."

Chapter Ninety-Six
The Golden Crust

———

When they arrived home, they did exactly as instructed.
Presumably some squad of witches, wizards and other authorities swarmed the place and shut it down, sweeping it for any sign of Society of All Magicks members and other villains. Perhaps all of that amid explosions and fire bombs, and earsplitting gunfire—or whatever the wizarding equivalent may be.

It can only be presumed because, unsurprisingly, all of them were sent to their beds, and they were allowed no further involvement in the matter.

Before bed, they briefed Puffin, then Dodder and Wimple, then some other officials. They told their story seven or eight times.

In between briefings, Madame Puffin conjured pizza from The Golden Crust. They ate enthusiastically—none more than Chase— and at every chance, hardly a word was spoken.

As Jack was finally lying down, the sun was rising through the curtained window of the room he and Chase had been given. It was only then that he realized almost everything he had been through— from the moment he had met Trygg—had happened only since he had awoken earlier that day in this very room. It would only be his second time sleeping in this bed. Amazing how so much could possibly happen in one or two days, but it had.

Before being sent to bed, Jack and Chase got in some hot water for leaving their beds in the first place. However, the next morning—afternoon, really—nothing more was said about that. There simply was too much else to discuss.

For one thing, Pesky was nowhere to be found.

Chapter Ninety-Seven
The Truth

——

In the afternoon, Jack awoke to find that Chase and Vidalia had already gotten up. Having slept much better than he thought he would be able to, he was in good spirits.

While he ate a simple breakfast at the kitchen table, Chase, Vidalia and Madame Puffin filled him in on what they knew, which was not much.

Madame Puffin looked terrible. She had dark puffy circles under her eyes, and her hair wilted from its normal grandeur. With everything over and done with, the Wargothe safely captured and all three kids back, Jack thought she would have gotten more sleep, but she was far from rested.

"Now that Jack is here to keep Chase involved," she said with a furtive glance at the boys, "There is, Vidalia dear, something we need resolved. Now please excuse us, boys, if you will. Vidalia, in the den the level of noise will be quieter still."

With that, she took Vidalia's hand and sauntered out of the room.

Jack and Chase were surprised but shrugged and continued talking. Mostly, they recapped the events of the night before. Chase asked questions about what Jack had gone through and then filled in the story from his own perspective.

It was not long before Jack heard Vidalia sobbing from the other room. Or, at least he thought he did. They quieted to see if they could make out any more, but heard nothing.

"Newt," Jack said abruptly soon after.

"What? Oh. I hate when you do that."

"I realized we haven't seen him since yesterday."

Neither had much inclination to see him and had nothing more to add to Jack's simple statement. Aside from a mental note to remember to ask Vidalia or Puffin about him, Jack shrugged and said no more about it.

About ten minutes later, Madame Puffin came back and sat down at the kitchen table with them. Vidalia was not with her, but Knocker, the kobold, followed behind and began pacing importantly, standing sentry at the entry to the kitchen. He gave Jack a quick wink and returned to his pacing.

Puffin gave a cheerless smile. "You boys are inseparable. Aren't you? You tell each other everything, true?"

"Sure."

"I guess so."

"Ok then, Chase, I'll let you stay but mostly so he won't have to repeat it. It will probably be easier that way, and besides, it might otherwise lose something in retreatment." She looked at the table, sadly.

"First I must explain, as Vidalia I have apprised—and I say with horrible disdain, and more than a little bit of surprise—that he's not been found anywhere; Pescipalius has gone missing. Of people there were many there, but his loss there's no dismissing."

"What?"

The boys were shocked. They had not expected that. "He's missing?"

Even Chase had worked out the meaning of her words.

"Sadly, it's true." She doodled absently with her fingertip on the table. It was obvious the news was hitting her hard.

"We suspect the Society, we do. But worry not. He will certainly be found, of that we've been assured. I'm convinced the police are bound to quickly get it all tidy and secured." Jack could see she was unconvinced herself, trying to make it easier on them, but she knew the truth of the matter. She was worried, that was clear.

"There was more I had to tell her—it simply couldn't wait. The timing is hardly stellar, yet the reasons carry cumbrous weight." Puffin took a deep breath and continued, "I had to inform her that indeed a Warlocke she is, sadly. Certainly, I could not mislead, but if to ease her burden, I would gladly."

Madame Puffin went on to explain, in her poetic way, that although she did not tell Vidalia outright, she is a smart girl and knew immediately what that meant. Vidalia is a Locke, not a Dorfnutter.

Although Jack could feel for Vidalia, it was better that she knew the truth now. He had felt immensely guilty that she had not believed Chase, and he knew at some point she would need to be convinced. Inside, he agreed the timing was terrible. He could not imagine being told that his father was missing, feared dead—and oh, by the way, he's not your real father.

Madame Puffin went on to explain that, yes, she had been the one to switch the babies at birth, but she'd had no choice. The prophecies told her that she must, but she was miserable at being the instrument of that particular prophecy.

"It's ok. Chase and I already know about the *Prophecy Untold*," he said, giving her a thin smile. It surprised Jack a little that she did not ask how they knew. She had bigger things on her mind—or given that she was a prophet, maybe she knew they would learn the truth long before they ever did.

Thinking like that made Jack dizzy.

He chanced a look in Knocker's direction. The little gremlin wore guilt across his brow but continued his silent pacing. Puffin exhaled deeply and looked Jack in the eyes. "Well, Jack, there is one more topic we must cover. Sadly, your past I must uncover."

Without intending to, he held his breath as she said, "As Vidalia, you are both Locke and Warlocke, it is true. I have sworn by my oath to tell both her and you. You, too, I switched that day—and I assure you not for grins, but the prophecy I could not betray, although it never once mentioned twins."

Chapter Ninety-Eight
The Whole Truth

J ack's head was spinning.

He was not certain if she said any more after that. He did not notice.

He did not have the capacity to.

With a ringing in his ears and a hot fuzziness across his face, it took him a moment before he realized he was saying "no" over and over again.

Yesterday he might have been excited to learn he was a Warlocke, but today he had his fill of that. Now he knew all too well what it meant—that his family was no longer his family, his home no longer his home. Losing all of that was too big a price to pay for a little excitement at being a Warlocke. Besides, he had gotten his taste of it and found it bitter.

"But, but ..." he sputtered uncontrollably. "But that can't be. You told me I was not the Warlocke, and you can't lie."

"I never told you that you were not. I simply said that a real Warlocke out there passes. Trust me, just then, you could not believe you were the hero for the masses. No matter what I said or did, it was not the time to convince you of your bid. Besides, you needed to believe you weren't important, with nothing up your sleeve except what you saw as short rent." She put her hand on his arm. "You needed to be yourself—better not to be thought through—knowing you are who you are, and not trying to be who you thought you ought to."

Somehow, he understood that. If he had known earlier that he was the Warlocke, would he have made some of the same decisions he ended up making? Probably not. He very well may not have been sitting in the kitchen at all if he had made different decisions. And things may not have turned out well for Vidalia or Chase either.

She was right. She had not lied. All she had said was that a Warlocke was out there. He had assumed the rest.

"But I have no magic." It was as much a question as not.

Madame Puffin smiled. "Is that what you think?" She looked directly into his eyes. "You have magic, of course. Never could you pass the brink if you'd had no magic source. The most certain proof lies right there in your hand," she said as Jack looked at the Fyrelocke, clutched tightly in his fist. "A human could not hold that without dying. You must have powerful magic to carry that brand. In fact, a goodly number of witches may themselves have died trying."

Suddenly it all flooded back to him. In Chase's room, the fyrestone had blown a hole in his floor as Chase was about to take it.

Ignatius had saved Chase's life.

In the cave, when Jack had first lifted the stone, he had collapsed immediately, overwhelmed by the sheer magic in the rock. Had it brought him to the very brink of his own death? Was that the cliff about which Madame Puffin had spoken later in the day?

Now he understood.

Even more, he understood the look witches gave the Fyrelocke as they held it. It was reverence. Maybe some part of it was their own personal validation that they were magic enough to hold it. They were good enough.

Ignatius' voice ran through his mind. *The magic is too much for people with not enough magic of their own. It would course through them like electricity and eat them alive. The shell of the geode only barely holds it together—it is the magic within you that controls it.*

Jack responded to him directly. *Why didn't you tell me that before? Why didn't you warn me before Chase tried to take the geode?*

Again, Ignatius spoke in that faint but clear voice only Jack could hear. *I couldn't. Nobody has ever communicated with the soul trapped within a fyrestone as you have. The best we might do is a spectral visit. This voice I now have was a gift from the puriform, and I didn't have it then.*

As Jack resumed his conversation with Madame Puffin, she explained how difficult and distasteful she had found the task of switching the babies. She almost could not bring herself to do it but knew that if she did not, the two shivering Locke babies would certainly die. She worried about the Dorfnutter baby, entrusted with John and Emily Locke, but what else could she do?

"But what happened to the real baby Jack, then?"

"A stillbirth he suffered," she said miserably. "But about that, your parents never knew. So true happiness you offered, even if the story wasn't perfectly true."

Chapter Ninety-Nine
Aftermath

T
he boys did end up missing one day of school, but neither complained.

Over the course of the next several weeks, a team tried to forensically reconstruct the entire series of events but found very little that Jack, Chase and Vidalia did not already know. In fact, the three were the source of much of what that team unearthed. They did soon learn that it was not just Pesky that went missing, but the whole of Wargothe Manor. In the spot where the house had been was nothing but a cleared field—a hole where the foundation and cellar had been.

The boy that Jack and Chase knew as Newt was also missing. When Puffin had gone to check on him earlier that morning, he had not been in his room and was nowhere to be found. The authorities were informed, but with everything else going on and so little to go by—nobody even knew his real name—Jack had to wonder how hard they would try to find him.

Jack and Vidalia had a lot of adjusting to do. Unquestionably, because Pesky was missing, Vidalia's adjustment was much harder. She walked around in a haze. Jack could only try to imagine her pain. He could not speak to his parents about any of this either, but at least they were not missing.

He did go back to live with the Boomershines—who were fine despite the spells they had suffered. They had no idea about the experiences Jack and Chase had and did not realize they had missed any time at all. They did not know what happened to their real son, or that Jack was not.

He vowed to never tell them.

He could get on with his family, his life, his inventions and his friends. Maybe he could begin to see his new sister differently. His cheeks burned red at how disagreeable he had considered her before, but now he would try his best to see her fairly. He could not even remember why they had argued so much.

That aside, he worried no more about the past. A Boomershine he may never genuinely be, but his parents did not need to know that. And with the Wargothe well and truly destroyed, there was no longer any threat to Jack, his friends, his family or his recently uncovered sister.

Certainly no threats of which he was aware.

Chapter One Hundred
Not Today

———

"**C**ome on. How do I do it? Do I throw it on the ground? Break it open?"

I have already told you what I will answer right now.

"I want to set you free," Jack said, as he had countless times since that day.

And I have answered you. Not today. Not yet.

The stone vibrated again, energy being drawn into the geode, as line on a fishing pole drawn into a spool. It always did this when Ignatius' ghost pulled itself back into the fyrestone—his way of saying that he would speak no more on the subject.

Not today.

ACKNOWLEDGMENTS

———

A great many helping hands went into the making of this novel. I wish to personally thank each of them for all the help and support they gave throughout the process. Thank you especially to my family, friends and beta readers (in alpha order): Ada Fredin, Chris Harte, Melissa Harte, Terry Harte, Jill Kusek, Finy Lazar, Justin Mostyn, Naomi Mostyn, Ryan Mostyn, Lea Panek, Susan Panek, Santosh Pinto, Rozshani V. Romero, Kim Schaefer, Kristie Scherer, Cyndi and Don Weiss, Madison Weiss and Virginia Weiss. They all provided great and valuable feedback. This novel is much better off for the thoughts they added.

My father and brother never got a chance to see this novel in print. Dad and Don, Chapter 24 is for you.

I would also like to thank Bill Greenleaf and Dave Baker for all their editorial wisdom. Without their help, this novel would have been less satisfying than a bowl of alphabet soup—and less nutritious.

In addition, a number of resources were used in order to produce this novel. I would be remiss if I did not thank them for their contributions, many without their own knowledge. The GIMP (GNU Image Manipulation Program) played a large part in allowing me to paint and design the cover and interior images. I truly want to thank the GIMP developers for helping me to fulfill certain parts of my vision. Thank you to font designers Manfred Klein (Aquiline and Ugly Qua), Backpacker (BPDots), Birgit Pulk (Kristi) and Steve Deffeyes (Gondola) for making your hard work available to designers everywhere. Thank you to the EOW (Englisc Onstigende Wordbōc) for helping me translate English into some very real Old English. Thanks to the stock image providers whose faces grace the interior picture of "Kee and Gina Cankrot": Tyler J. Green and Ashley Luttrell. Finally, a thank you to the town of Brighton and Hove, some of the history of which is loosely referenced here.

ABOUT THE AUTHOR

R. Christopher Kobb lives in the
Chicago area with his daughter.

An avid writer and artist, this is his
first novel.

✳

To learn more about upcoming
events and new releases, go to
www.rckobb.com

219 1 1 1 22 7 3 1 195 8 1 3 114 3 1 5 123 7 2 7 138 6 3 1 20 5 2 3 82 3 1 1
132 1 1 10 192 5 1 19 192 5 1 20 2 5 4 9 164 7 4 25 89 5 1 9 143 1 1 4 105 7 6
7 171 8 2 6 43 2 4 5 77 4 1 5 77 2 1 14 257 3 1 12 186 1 7 4 51 1 1 1 67 13 5 4